# THE BIRDS

"The Birds is a masterpiece, one of the greatest comedies ever written and probably Aristophanes' finest. Splendidly lyrical, shot through with gentle Utopian satire and touched by the sadness of the human condition, its ironic gaiety and power of invention never flag; in no other play is Aristophanes' comic vision so comprehensively or lovingly at odds with the world."

*Thus William Arrowsmith describes the play he has so memorably translated into vivid modern English. In this wondrous portrayal of a flawed utopia called Cloudcuckooland, Aristophanes offers an enchanting escape into the world of free-flying fantasy—and a mind-expanding mirror in which are reflected the eternal dilemmas of man on earth.*

WILLIAM ARROWSMITH was born in New Jersey in 1924, and received degrees from Princeton and Oxford Universities. He has been a Rhodes Scholar, a Woodrow Wilson Fellow, a Guggenheim Fellow, and the recipient of the Prix de Rome as well as numerous other distinguished awards. Not only has Professor Arrowsmith won recognition as one of the foremost classical teachers, scholars, and translators in the English-speaking world, he also has been a prime mover and shaper of the dramatic resurgence of the art of translation witnessed in America in recent years.

# THE BIRDS

## By Aristophanes

*Translated by* WILLIAM ARROWSMITH

THE MENTOR GREEK COMEDY
*General Editor:* WILLIAM ARROWSMITH

A MENTOR BOOK
NEW AMERICAN LIBRARY
TIMES MIRROR
NEW YORK AND SCARBOROUGH, ONTARIO
THE NEW ENGLISH LIBRARY LIMITED, LONDON

# FOR JEAN

 MENTOR TRADEMARK REG. U.S. PAT. OFF. AND FOREIGN COUNTRIES
REGISTERED TRADEMARK—MARCA REGISTRADA
HECHO EN CHICAGO, U.S.A.

SIGNET, SIGNET CLASSICS, MENTOR, PLUME, MERIDIAN AND NAL BOOKS are published in the United States by The New American Library, Inc., 1633 Broadway, New York, New York 10019, in Canada by The New American Library of Canada Limited, 81 Mack Avenue, Scarborough, Ontario M1L 1M8, in the United Kingdom by The New English Library Limited, Barnard's Inn, Holborn, London, EC1N 2JR, England

FIRST MENTOR PRINTING, MARCH, 1970

5  6  7  8  9  10  11  12  13

PRINTED IN CANADA

# CONTENTS

# Introduction

## The Play and Its Interpretation

Nobody denies that *The Birds* is a masterpiece, one of the greatest comedies ever written and probably Aristophanes' finest. Splendidly lyrical, shot through with gentle Utopian satire and touched by the sadness of the human condition, its ironic gaiety and power of invention never flag; in no other play is Aristophanes' comic vision so comprehensively or lovingly at odds with his world.

But if the play is by common consent a great one, there is little agreement about what it means. Thus it has, with great ingenuity and small cogency, been interpreted as a vast, detailed comic allegory of the Sicilian expedition: Pisthetairos stands for Alkibiades; Hoopoe is the general Lamachos; the Birds are Athenians, the gods Spartans, and so on. Alternatively, the play has been viewed as Aristophanes' passionate appeal for the reform and renewal of Athenian public life under the leadership of the noble Pisthetairos, a true Aristophanic champion cut from the same cloth as Dikaiopolis in *The Acharnians*. Again, probably in revenge for so much unlikely ingenuity, it has been claimed that *The Birds* is best understood as a fantastic escapist extravaganza created as a revealing antidote to the prevalent folly of Athenian political life. And, with the exception of the word "escapist," this last view seems to me essentially correct. But whatever else *The Birds* may be, it is not escapist.

Any translation worth the name necessarily involves an interpretation, and it is my hope that my version will make my interpretation clear and convincing. But because in some respects my view of the play is unorthodox and this is crucial to the interpretation, I offer the following points for the reader's consideration.

1) *The life of The Birds.* Like many Aristophanic comedies, *The Birds* takes its title from its chorus; but unlike, say, *Wasps*, which is based upon a simple simile (jurors are waspish: they buzz, swarm, sting, etc.), *Birds* and *Clouds* are titles around which cluster a great many traditional associations, idioms, and ideas. Thus in *Clouds* the chorus symbolizes the Murky Muse, that inflated, shining, insubstantial, and ephemeral power which inspires sophists, dithyrambic poets, prophets, and other pompous frauds. Similarly, in *Birds* there is the same natural clustering of association and standard idiom, and the associations are crucial to the play's understanding. On the most natural level, of course, the life of the Birds symbolizes precisely what one would expect: the simple, uncomplicated rustic life of peace. But behind this natural symbolism, deepening it and particularizing it, lies the chronic and pervasive escape-symbolism of late fifth-century Athens. In play after play of Euripides, for instance, chorus and characters alike, when confronted by the anguish of tragic existence, cry out their longing to escape, to be a bird, a fact of which Aristophanes makes extensive use, shaping his play around the symptomatic mortal infatuation with the birds. It is for this reason, this pervasive hunger for escape from intolerable existence which haunts tragedy and society alike, that Aristophanes makes his Birds address his audience with words of tragic pathos:

> *O suffering mankind,*
> > *lives of twilight,*
> > > *race feeble and fleeting*
> > *like the leaves scattered!*
> > > *Pale generations,*
> > > > *creatures of clay,*
> > *the wingless, the fading!*
> > > *Unhappy mortals,*
> > > > *shadows in time,*
> > *flickering dreams!*
> > > *Hear us now,*
> > > > *the ever-living Birds,*
> > *the undying,*
> > > *the ageless ones,*
> > > > *scholars of eternity.*

And these lines in their turn look forward to the ironic apotheosis of the mortal Pisthetairos with which the play closes. Mankind's crazy comic dream is a wish-fulfillment darkened by death. But the dream survives.

My point is this: far from writing an escapist extravaganza, Aristophanes dramatizes the ironic fulfillment in divinity of the Athenian man who wants to escape. What begins as hunger for the simple life ends—such is the character of Athenians and true men—in world-conquest and the defeat of the gods; or it would end there, if only it could. This is the *hybris* of enterprise and daring, the trait from which no Athenian can ever escape. Aristophanes' irony is, I think, loving.

2) *The Theme.* It is commonly said that *The Birds* is unlike other Aristophanic comedies in having no pointed central theme or particular concern (e.g., peace in *Acharnians* and *Peace;* demagoguery in *Knights,* sophistry in *Clouds,* etc.), and at first blush this seems to be true. But unless I am badly mistaken, the central concern of the play is less noticeable only because it is more comprehensive, including in itself most of the targets of the earlier plays. That concern is *polupragmosunē*, a concept which Athenians used as a general description of their most salient national characteristics. At its broadest *polupragmosunē* is that quality of spectacular restless energy that made the Athenians both the glory and the bane of the Hellenic world. On the postive side, it connotes energy, enterprise, daring, ingenuity, originality, and curiosity; negatively it means restless instability, discontent with one's lot, persistent and pointless busyness, meddling interference, and mischievous love of novelty. The Athenian Empire itself is a visible creation of political *polupragmosunē*, and so too are the peculiar liabilities to which empire made the Athenians subject: the love of litigation, the susceptibility to informers and demagogues, the violent changes in national policy and, most stunning example of all, the Sicilian expedition. In political terms, *polupragmosunē* is the very spirit of Athenian imperialism, its remorseless need to expand, the *hybris* of power and energy in a spirited people; in moral terms, it is a divine discontent and an impatience with necessity, a disease whose symptoms are disorder, corruption, and the hunger for change.

Athens with its *polupragmosunē* is unbearable for Pisthetairos and Euelpides, and so, rational escapists both, they set out to find among the Birds precisely what they miss in

Athens: the quiet, leisurely, simple, uncomplicated peace-loving life of the Birds, which is called *apragmosunē.* Confronted by the hostility of the Birds to man, Pisthetairos ingeniously conceives the idea of Cloudcuckooland. And from this point on, totally forgetting his quest for *apragmosunē,* he becomes the open and skillful exponent of *polupragmosunē:* persuasive, ingenious, cunning, meddlesome, and imperialistic. The characterization could hardly be more explicit or the change more deliberate, as the peace-loving escapist, with ruthless policy and doubtful arguments, pushes ahead with his scheme for the New Athens of the Birds. It is both comic and ironic, and Aristophanes' point is that no Athenian can escape his origins. His character is *polupragmosunē,* and character is destiny, as Herakleitos said. Put an Athenian among the Birds, and he will be an imperialist with wings and fight with gods.

3) *Pisthetairos.* It is sometimes said—quite wrongly, I believe—that Aristophanes' characters move on a single plane, without depth or complexity. If I am right, Pisthetairos' character, like Dikaiopolis' and Strepsiades', displays itself in action, not in professions; its basic simplicity, the thrust for power, is not something given but something defined in action. Like Dikaiopolis and Strepsiades, he *realizes* his name; but whereas Dikaiopolis' purpose is good and his methods roguish, Pisthetairos has no purpose but power and his methods are the appropriate ones. He compels assent and even admiration, as politicians do, by sheer persuasiveness and virtuosity and energy, but the energy is the dither of power for its own sake, without a rational goal in sight, restless and unappeasable: sheer *polupragmosunē.* He is Aristophanes' example of a politician without a policy, or nearly without one, unless we count to his credit his success in protecting Cloudcuckooland from ravenous interlopers, gods, and other pests.

4) *Cloudcuckooland.* Like Pisthetairos, Cloudcuckooland itself is treated ironically. On the one hand it is a pipedream Utopia from which a few of the nuisances and spongers that infest cities are driven out by an enraged Pisthetairos; on the other it is, especially in the methods of its founding, a visible parody of the Athenian Empire. Historical parallels and allusions here can be overdone, but I wonder what Athenian could have failed to notice the way in which, point for point, the policies and strategies of imperial Athens toward the member-

states of her empire are adapted to Cloudcuckooland's campaign against the gods. Pisthetairos specifically proposes to exterminate the gods by "Melian starvation," and the general proposals of boycott vividly recall the Megarian Decree. Also pertinent, I think, is the close resemblance between Pisthetairos and the Birds and Athens and her subject-cities, once her allies: slowly the Birds, like the allies, yield to the initiative of the stronger, putting their strength at the service of another intellect, thereby losing their freedom. It is Aristophanes' point that the Birds, like the allies, are stupid; Athens and Pisthetairos clever and unscrupulous. And significantly, I think, the play closes with a light irony as Pisthetairos and the gods prepare to celebrate their truce with a dinner of—poultry; jailbirds, true, but birds for all that. It is, for the Birds, an ominous sign of things to come. All their campaign against the gods has brought them is a new tyrant, no less voracious than the old and just as treacherous.

But if Cloudcuckooland serves to parody the growth of Athenian power and imperialistic politics, it also serves as a convenient and satisfying appeal for Athens to renew herself by ridding the city of the informers, sponges, charlatans, sophists, bureaucracy, and abuses that have made it almost unliveable. Irony here crosses with irony, as Pisthetairos, the champion of *polupragmosunē*, beats out the rival champions. So too, in *Knights*, the improbable cause of Demos' resurgence is none other than the tripe-peddling demagogue who has out-Kleoned Kleon.

5) *The Apotheosis.* In Aristophanes' eyes the logical terminus of Athenian restlessness and aggressiveness is that man should become god, wear wings and rule the world. The blasphemy is prevented only by the impossibility of its realization. But the ambition survives and luxuriates in man's discontent with his condition, his mortal *hybris*. For Aristophanes that discontent was tragic and meant man's loss of his only possible happiness: peace lost in war, traditional dignity swallowed up in the restless greed for wealth and power, honor lost in the inhumanity of imperialism and political tyranny. But he also knew that such discontent was born of life and aggressive hunger for larger life.

## Date and Circumstances

*The Birds* was first performed at the Great Dionysia in late March, 414 B.C. and was awarded the Second Prize. The First Prize was taken by Ameipsias with his *Komastai* ("The Revellers") and the Third Prize by Phrynichos with his *Monotropos* ("The Hermit"). The year preceding the play's performance, during its composition, must have been a grim and bitter time in Athens, especially for an exponent of peace and rational politics like Aristophanes. In May, 415, just as the Athenian fleet was about to sail for Sicily on its disastrous expedition, the entire city was thrown into a superstitious panic by the mutilation of the pillars of Hermes, the work either of drunken carousers or of a political faction bent on discrediting Alkibiades, the commander of the Sicilian expedition. As a result, the whole expedition seemed to hang under a heavy cloud; accusations were being made on all sides, and the general atmosphere of the city was one of suspicion, horror, and frenetic political activity. Finally, after the fleet had sailed, evidence was found which seemed to incriminate Alkibiades and a state galley was sent out with orders to bring him back to Athens to stand trial. It is unlikely that Alkibiades' escape and defection to Sparta were known at Athens at the time the play was performed.

## The Translation

This translation is meant to provide a faithful, but not a literal, version of *The Birds*. Literalness in any case is out of the question: a literal Aristophanes would be both unreadable and unplayable, and therefore unfaithful. But fidelity is clearly a matter of degree and relation: *how* faithful and faithful to *what?*

It was my purpose to create a lively, contemporary acting version of the play, a translation which might also, I hoped, be read for pleasure or study, and which would be as loyal to

Greek and Greek experience as I could make it without involving myself in disloyalty to English. Only by so doing, I thought, could I remain faithful to two languages and two cultures at the same time. For the same reason I have deliberately avoided wholly modernizing or "adapting" the play. If the diction of this version is essentially contemporary American English, its experience, I believe, is basically Athenian. Some modernization, of course, was not only inevitable but also desirable. But generally I have preferred to suggest the similarities between Athens and America without asserting, or forcing, an identity. If the language does its work, the experience should translate itself with only a little occasional help from the translator. Or so I thought.

For fidelity's sake, this is also a poetic version. A prose Aristophanes is to my mind as much a monstrosity as a limerick in prose paraphrase. And for much the same reasons. If Aristophanes is visibly obscene, farcical, and colloquial, he is also lyrical, elegant, fantastic, and witty. And a translation which, by flattening incongruities and tensions, reduces one dimension necessarily reduces the other. Bowdlerize Aristophanes and you sublimate him into something less vital and whole; prose him and you cripple his wit, dilute his obscenity and slapstick, and weaken his classical sense of the wholeness of human life.

Translating comedy is necessarily very different from translating tragedy; not only is it more demanding, but its principles, because they are constantly being improvised or modified, are harder to state. Insofar as I can describe them or deduce them from my own practice, my general principles are these:

1) *Meter.*    Aristophanes' basic dialogue line is a loose, colloquial iambic hexameter (*senarii*), and my English equivalent is a loose five-stress line. It was my opinion that the flexibility required by the Greek could best be achieved by a meter capable of modulating, without jarring or unnaturalness, back to the norm of English dramatic verse, the blank. At its most humdrum such a line is indistinguishable from prose, but worked up, patterned with regular stresses, it can readily be traditionalized as tragic parody or cant or realized as speakable poetry in its own right. The longer anapestic and trochaic lines I have rendered by a six-beat movement (except in the first

section of the *parabasis*, where I have adapted William Carlos Williams' triplet-line to my own purposes). Because the convention of *stichomythia* seemed deadening when brought over into English and served no useful dramatic purpose, I have everywhere taken the liberty of breaking it down.

2) *Obscenity*.  I have refused on principle to bowdlerize. Equally, I have tried to avoid the quicksands of archness or cuteness on the one hand and sledgehammer shock-tactics on the other. Where Aristophanes is blunt, I have left him blunt, but generally I have tried to realize his rhetorical obscenities with the elegance and neatness that might make them truly obscene.

3) *Stage Directions*.   The Greek plays have come down to us almost entirely without stage directions. To some small degree they are supplied by the ancient scholiasts, but because this is an acting version of the play and because comedy constantly suggests and requires stage action, I have freely supplied stage directions. Wherever possible, I have relied on indications in the text, but when a direction was clearly required and the text offered no help, I have used my imagination.

4) *Improvisation*.   There are occasions (e.g., a pun, an obscure reference, or a tangle of politics, pun and idiom) when the Greek is simply untranslatable. On such occasions it has been my practice to improvise (see, for instance, the note on p. 140. *Her lover*), on the grounds that literal translation would have slowed or obscured the dramatic situation, and this is fatal to comedy. Normally I have indicated when I have improvised and why. But I should also confess that there are a few passages in which I have improvised on my own, without warrant. My only excuse is the self-indulgent one that I thought they might be justified as compensation for losses elsewhere.

5) *Tragic and Poetic Parody*.   Aristophanes constantly parodies tragedy and poetry, and these parodies were meant to be recognized. Since modern audiences cannot be expected to recognize them—especially since most of the originals are no longer extant—the translator is required to do the impossible and create the illusion of parody. This means in effect that the parodies must be so grotesque as to be instantly recognizable

as parody, and to this end I have deliberately heightened fustian, archaism, and bombast. Thus the Poet in this play speaks a parody of Pindar that is sheer doggerel and utterly un-Pindaric. I can only plead that my purpose was not to slander Pindar but to make the Poet an obvious hack.

6) *Dialects and Nonsense.* Aristophanic comedy abounds with dialects—Skythian policemen, Spartan heralds, sham Persians, Boiotians, Megarians, and the pure jabberwocky god of *The Birds*, Triballos. Because these dialects seemed to me both comic and conventional, I have everywhere rendered them by an apposite contemporary comic dialect: mint-julep Southern, broad Brooklynese, Katzenjammerkids German, etc. Nothing, in my opinion, is less comic or more tiresome than dialectal realism; for comedy, a recognizable *comic* convention is required, whatever the cost in anachronism. In the case of Triballos, who speaks pure nonsense, I have preferred to invent some genuine English nonsense rather than transliterate his Greekish gibberish. Herakles, it should be noted, does *not* in the original speak a dialect at all, but his hungry lowbrow character seemed to me to require conventional treatment, and I accordingly arranged it.

7) *Rhetorical Conventions and Jargon.* What is true of dialects is also true of professional rhetoric and jargon: if they are to be comic, they have to be translated into an apposite convention of English rhetoric or jargon. Invariably, this means that their language must be heightened and made even more ponderous than it is in the Greek. The astronomer Meton, for instance, is used by Aristophanes to parody the jargon and abstruse pomposity of sophistic science. But because Greek scientific jargon was a relatively immature growth (at least when compared with the jargons of modern science), his words, literally translated, sound to modern ears merely somewhat silly. In the circumstances I deliberately heightened his language, adding technical terms and jargonizing it further, in the belief that only by so doing could I create the effect of gobbledegook that Meton's demonstration was intended to have for Athenian ears.

8) *Personal and Topical Allusions.* Aristophanes' frequent allusions to persons and events present the translator with a ticklish problem. Some of them are so obscure as to be mean-

ingless to anybody but a prosopographer; others exist because they offer happy opportunities for puns or gibes at topical personalities; still others are crucial to the play's meaning. In general, it has been my practice to simplify, suppressing totally obscure allusions (see, for instance, the note on p. 135, *this stinking, jabbering Magpie here*) altogether, and avoiding such cumbersome and evasive phrases as "you know who I mean" and the like. In the first case, it seemed important not to slow the action on a minor obscurity; in the second, no allusion at all seemed preferable to an unsatisfactory echo of one. But where names and events seemed essential to the meaning, I have retained them, wherever possible intruding a gloss which might minimize the difficulty even though it expanded the text. So far as I know, every suppressed allusion is mentioned and explained in the notes.

## Text and Acknowledgments

The texts on which I have chiefly relied for this translation are those of R. Cantarella and Victor Coulon (Budé), supplemented by the Oxford text of Hall and Geldart. Like every modern English or American translator of Aristophanes, I have derived invaluable aid and comfort from the splendid text and commentary of Benjamin Bickley Rogers.

For suggestions, corrections, and *trouvailles* I owe thanks to colleagues and friends too many to mention. But my chief mentor has been my wife. It was she who endured with unflinching patience and even good humor the successive versions, and it is to her, as orniphile and critic, that this translation is dedicated.

Finally, I should like to thank both the Yaddo Corporation and the American Academy in Rome for grants of money and leisure which made this translation possible, and the Research Institute of the University of Texas for secretarial assistance.

*Austin, Texas*                                    WILLIAM ARROWSMITH

# Characters of the Play

EUELPIDES
   (*i.e., Hopeful*), *an Athenian*
PISTHETAIROS
   (*i.e., Plausible*), *an Athenian*
SANDPIPER,
   *servant of Epops the Hoopoe*
EPOPS, or HOOPOE,
   *otherwise known as Tereus*
CHORUS OF BIRDS
KORYPHAIOS
*1* PRIEST
*2* POET          } the visiting
*3* PROPHET         magpie
*4* METON
*5* INSPECTOR
*6* LEGISLATOR
FIRST MESSENGER
SENTRY
IRIS
HERALD
DELINQUENT
KINESIAS,
   *a dithyrambic poet*
INFORMER
PROMETHEUS
POSEIDON
TRIBALLOS
HERAKLES
SECOND MESSENGER

SCENE: *A desolate wilderness.\* In the background is a single tree and the sheer rock-face of a cliff. Enter, in the last stages of exhaustion, Euelpides and Pisthetairos. On his arm Euelpides carries a Magpie; Pisthetairos holds a Crow. They are followed by slaves with their luggage, consisting mostly of kitchen equipment, cauldrons, pots, spits, etc.*

17

EUELPIDES

*To his Magpie.*

Straight ahead, croaker? Over by that tree?

PISTHETAIROS

Damn this cracked Crow! He keeps cawing me backwards.

EUELPIDES

Look, halfwit, what's the point of hiking these hills?
If we don't stop this zigzagging pretty soon,
I'm through.

PISTHETAIROS

                I must have been mad—trusting a Crow
to go trudging off on this hundred-mile hike.

EUELPIDES

                                    *You*'re mad?
Look at me, man—hitched to a Magpie
and my toenails worn away right down to the nub.

PISTHETAIROS

I'll be damned if I know where we are.

EUELPIDES

                            Say,
do you suppose we could find our way back home from
here?

PISTHETAIROS

Friend, even Exekestides couldn't do *that*.*

EUELPIDES

*Stumbling.*

                                Hell.

PISTHETAIROS

That's just where we're headed now, old man.

**EUELPIDES**

> You know,
> that birdseller Philokrates who sold us these damn Birds
> was a filthy fraud, that's what. Swearing up and down
> that these two Birds here would lead us to the Hoopoe,
> old Tereus the Bird who used to be a man,*
> and swindling us with this stinking, jabbering Magpie here*
> for two bits and that cluckhead Crow of yours for six!
> And what do they do but nip our fingers off?

*To the Magpie.*

> Well, what are you gaping at, imbecile? Where?
> Straight into the cliff? But there's no road there, idiot.

**PISTHETAIROS**

> A *road*? Sweet gods, there isn't even a track!

**EUELPIDES**

> Say, isn't your Crow croaking something about a road?

**PISTHETAIROS**

> You know, now that you mention it, I think he *is* croaking
> in a different key.

**EUELPIDES**

> Something about a road, isn't it?

**PISTHETAIROS**

> Naw, he's cawing he'll gnaw my fingers off.

**EUELPIDES**

> It's a filthy shame, that's what. Think of it, man:
> here we are dying to go tell it to the Birds,*
> and then, by god, we can't even find the way.

*To the Audience.*

> Yes, dear people, we confess we're completely mad.
> But it's not like Sakas'* madness. Not a bit.
> For he, poor dumb foreigner, wants in, while we,

born and bred Athenians both, true blue,
true citizens, not afraid of any man,
want out.
            Yes, we've spread our little feet
and taken off. Not that we hate Athens—
heavens, no. And not that dear old Athens
isn't grand, that blessed land where men are free—
to pay their taxes.*

            No, look to the locust
who, one month or two, drones and shrills
among the little thickets, while the men of Athens,
perched upon the thorny thickets of the law, sit
shrilling out their three score years and ten.
Because of legal locusts,* gentlemen, we have left,
lugging these baskets and pots and boughs of myrtle,
looking for some land of soft and lovely leisure*
where a man may loaf and play and settle down
for good. Tereus the Hoopoe is our journey's end.
From him we hope to learn if he has seen
in all his many travels such a place
on earth.

**PISTHETAIROS**

        Pssst! Hey!

**EUELPIDES**

            What's up?

**PISTHETAIROS**

                        Look at my Crow
staring up in the air.

**EUELPIDES**

            And my Magpie's gaping too.
It looks as though he's pointing his beak at the sky.
I'll bet that means there's Birds somewhere hereabouts.
We'll find out soon enough if we make a ruckus.

**PISTHETAIROS**

I know. Try kicking the side of the cliff with your foot.*

**EUELPIDES**

Go bash it with your head. You'll make more noise.

**PISTHETAIROS**

Pick up a rock and pound.

**EUELPIDES**

Good idea. I'll try.

*He picks up a rock and pounds on the cliff, shouting.*

Boy! Hey, boy!

**PISTHETAIROS**

Don't call old Hoopoe "boy."
You'd better say, "Ho, Hoopoe!" or "Hey, Epops!"

**EUELPIDES**

Hey, Hoopoe!

*No answer.*

Hmmm. Shall I try him again?
Yoohoo, Hoopoe!

*A concealed door in the cliff suddenly swings open and a Sand-piper with an enormous curved beak peers out, almost spitting Pisthetairos.*

**SANDPIPER**

What are you whooping about?

**EUELPIDES**

Apollo help us! What a beak on the Bird!

*In his fright he lets go of his Magpie who flaps off. Pisthetairos falls backward, losing his Crow, while the Sandpiper retreats in horror.*

**SANDPIPER**

Halp!

Nest-robbers! Egg-stealers! Bird-catchers!

Halp!

EUELPIDES

You hear that? His bark is worse than his beak.

SANDPIPER

Mortals, you die!

EUELPIDES

But we're not men.

SANDPIPER

What are you?

EUELPIDES

Me? I'm *turdus turdus*. An African migrant.*

SANDPIPER

What nonsense.

EUELPIDES

Not nonsense, crap. Look at my feet.

SANDPIPER

*Indicating Pisthetairos.*

And that bird over there? What's his species?

PISTHETAIROS

Me?

Brown-tailed Smellyrump. Quail family.

EUELPIDES

*To Sandpiper.*

Say,
what about you, Birdie? What the hell are you?

SANDPIPER

I'm a Slavebird.*

EUELPIDES

I see. Some bantam thrash you
in a scrap?

SANDPIPER

No, but when the boss got himself changed
into a Hoopoe, I put in my application for feathers too
so I could stay in his service, doing odd jobs and buttling.

EUELPIDES

And since when have our Birds been having butlers?

SANDPIPER

He gets the habit, I think, from having once been human.
But suppose he wants some sardines. Up I jump,
dash down with a dish and catch him some fish.
If it's soup he wants, I grab a little ladle
and skitter to the kettle.

EUELPIDES

Quite the runner, eh?
Tell you what, runner-bird: just skitter inside
and fetch your master out.

SANDPIPER

But he's napping now.
He gorged himself silly on a mess of midges and myrtle.

EUELPIDES

His nap be damned. Go wake him.

SANDPIPER

I warn you:
He'll be grumpy. But just for a favor I'll do it.

*Exit Sandpiper.*

**PISTHETAIROS**

And then drop dead.

*To Euelpides.*

—Whoosh, I'm still shaking.

**EUELPIDES**

Me too. And guess what. My Magpie's gone,
got clear away.

**PISTHETAIROS**

*Got away?* Why you big baby,
were you so scared you dropped your load?

**EUELPIDES**

Well,
what about you? Where's your bird?

**PISTHETAIROS**

Where's my bird?
Right here in my hand.*

**EUELPIDES**

Right where?

**PISTHETAIROS**

Well, he was here.

**EUELPIDES**

And where were you? Holding on for dear life?

**HOOPOE**

*From within.*

CLEAR THE COPSE, I SAY, AND WHEEL ME OUT!

*The eccyclema wheels out the Hoopoe, sitting on a pile of
brush and peering out from a thicket. Except for his huge crest
and beak and a few bedraggled feathers here and there, the
Hoopoe is human.*

EUELPIDES

Holy Herakles! That's no Bird, it's a freak.
Get a load of that plumage! What a tiara!

HOOPOE

Who *are* you?

EUELPIDES

      Birdie, you looked bedraggled.
I'll bet the gods\* gave you some nasty knocks.

HOOPOE

You dare sneer at my plumage? I, strangers,
was once a man.

EUELPIDES

        Oh, we're not laughing at you.

HOOPOE

Then, what's so funny?

EUELPIDES

          Your beak. It tickles me.

HOOPOE

I am dressed as the poet Sophokles disfigures me\*
in that atrocious tragedy of his entitled *Tereus*.

EUELPIDES

                *Gee*,
*you*'re Tereus in person?
          Are you Bird or Peacock?

HOOPOE

*With ferocious dignity.*

I am a Bird.

EUELPIDES

      Then what happened to your feathers, Bird?

HOOPOE

They've fallen out.

EUELPIDES

Caught the mange, I suppose?

HOOPOE

I'll ignore that remark.
All Birds moult in winter,*
and then in spring we grow fresh feathers back.
Now then, suppose you tell me who *you* are.

EUELPIDES

Mortals.

HOOPOE

Country?

EUELPIDES

Athens, land of lovely—warships.

HOOPOE

Then you must be jurymen.*

EUELPIDES

No, just the reverse:
we're non-jurymen.

HOOPOE

I thought that species had become extinct
in Athens.

EUELPIDES

You can still find a few growing wild—*
if you look hard enough.

HOOPOE

But what brings you here, gentlemen?

**EUELPIDES**

Your assistance and advice.

**HOOPOE**

My advice? About what?

**EUELPIDES**

You were mortal once as we are mortal now.
You once were plagued with creditors, and we're plagued now.
You welshed on your debts; we welsh on our debts now.
But though you were mortal once, you became a Bird
and flew the circuit of the spreading earth and sea;
yet both as Bird and Man you understand.
And so we come to you, to ask your help,
bearing our hope that you may know some land,
some country like a blanket, soft and snug,*
between whose folds two tired men might flop.

**HOOPOE**

And Athens won't do? You want something more . . .
splendid?

**EUELPIDES**

It wasn't exactly splendor we had in mind. No,
we wanted a country that was made for just *us*.

**HOOPOE**

Ah, something more exclusive? An Aristocracy perhaps?

**EUELPIDES**

Ugh. Can't abide that Aristokrates.

**HOOPOE**

But my dear fellow,
what *do* you want?

**EUELPIDES**

Oh, the sort of country
where the worst trouble I could have would be

friends trooping to my door bright and early
in the morning to pester me with invitations to dinner:
"C'mon, old boy, I'm throwing a big celebration.
So fresh up, give your kiddies a bath,
and come on over. And don't go standing me up,
or I won't turn to you when I'm in trouble."

HOOPOE

Zeus, you like your troubles pleasant, don't you?

*To Pisthetairos.*

And you?

PISTHETAIROS

  I like pleasant troubles too.

HOOPOE

         For instance?

PISTHETAIROS

For instance, this. Some pretty little boy's old man
comes up, really peeved, giving me hell:
"Fine way you treat my son, you old stinker!
You met the boy coming home from the baths
and never fondled him, never even kissed him
or tickled his balls. And *you*, his daddy's pal!"

HOOPOE

Poor old bastard, you *are* in love with trouble.
Well, I've got just the place to please you both.
Now, down on the Red Sea—

EUELPIDES

        Sweet gods, not the sea!
No, sir. I don't want any court-officials with summons*
and subpoenas showing up on ships at the crack of dawn.
Look here, don't you know of some city in Hellas?

HOOPOE

Well now, there's always Lepreus? How would that suit you?

**EUELPIDES**

Lepreus? Never heard of it. Offhand, I'd say no.
Smacks of old Melanthios. He's leprous.

**HOOPOE**

                              Hmmm.
Well, how about Opous then?

**EUELPIDES**

                    Count me out.
If Opountios comes from Opous,* then Opous
isn't for me. You couldn't pay me to live there.
But look here, what kind of life do you Birds lead?
You should know. You've lived here long enough.

**HOOPOE**

Life among the Birds? Not bad. And you don't need cash.

**EUELPIDES**

Well, that's the worst of life's big swindles disposed of.

**HOOPOE**

We scour the gardens for food, pecking mint,
scrabbling for poppyseed, sesame and myrtle-berries . . .

**EUELPIDES**

Gods alive, that's not life! That's a honeymoon!*

**PISTHETAIROS**    *a new twist*

*Suddenly illuminated.*

WAIT!
        WONDERFUL!
                I'VE GOT IT!
                        WHAT A SCHEME!
If you Birds will just do what I say, we'll make it succeed.

**HOOPOE**

Do what?

PISTHETAIROS

First, take my advice. For instance,
stop flapping around with your beaks hanging open.
It looks undignified and people jeer at the Birds.
In Athens whenever we see some silly ass,
we ask, "Hey, who's that Bird? and people say,*
"Oh, *him?* He's a real bat, dumb as a dodo,
booby, that's what, hasn't got the brains of a Bird."

HOOPOE

A palpable hit. And we deserve it too.
But what remedy do you suggest?

PISTHETAIROS

Found your own city.

HOOPOE    *the plot*

Found *our own city?* But who ever heard
of a City of Birds?

PISTHETAIROS

O Hebetude, thy name is Hoopoe!
Look down there.

HOOPOE

I'm looking.

PISTHETAIROS

Now look up there.

HOOPOE

I'm looking.

PISTHETAIROS

Way up. Crane your neck.

HOOPOE

By Zeus,
I'll be a helluva sight if I sprain my neck looking.

**PISTHETAIROS**

See anything?

**HOOPOE**

Nothing but clouds and a mess of sky.

**PISTHETAIROS**

Precisely. That mess of sky is the sphere of the Birds.

**HOOPOE**

Sphere? How do you mean?

**PISTHETAIROS**

Habitat, as it were.
The heavens, you see, revolve upon a kind of pole*
or axis, whence we call the sky a sphere.
Well then, you settle in your sphere, you build your walls,
and from this sphere of yours a city will appear.
And then, my friend, you'll be lords of all mankind
as once you were merely lords of locusts and bugs.
As for the gods, if they object or get in your way,
you can wipe them all out by starvation.*

**HOOPOE**

Wipe them out?
But *how?*

**PISTHETAIROS**

Your air is the boundary between earth and heaven.
Now just as we, when we make a trip to Delphi,
are required to secure a visa from the Theban government,
so you, when men propose a sacrifice to heaven,
impose a boycott, refusing your passport to these offerings
and forbidding any transit through your land,
until the gods agree to pay you tribute.

**HOOPOE**

By Earth!
Holy Snares! Sweep Springes and Nets!
A trickier gimmick I never heard of yet!

We'll put it to a vote. A referendum. We'll enlist your help
and build our city, provided the Birds agree.

PISTHETAIROS

But who will make the motion?

HOOPOE

You, of course.
Don't worry. They don't twitter nonsense any more.
They used to chirp, but now I've taught them Greek.

PISTHETAIROS

But can we muster a quorum?

HOOPOE

Nothing simpler.
I'll just step behind this little thicket here
and wake my sleeping wife, my lovely Nightingale.
We'll do a small duet and whistle them here.
They'll all come flocking in when they hear our song.

PISTHETAIROS

Hoopoe, old Bird, you're wonderful!
But hurry. Quick.
Go wake your sleeping Nightingale and sing your song.

*The Hoopoe retires and begins to sing.*

HOOPOE

Awake from sleep, my love!
Sing, O tawnythroat,
bird with honeyed tongue!
Awake and sing
your song and mine,
*Itys,   Itys!*

*From the thicket the flute begins its obbligato in imitation of
the song of the Nightingale at her most melancholy.*

Pure sound of sorrow!
Hear it rise,

a grief that goes,
> *Itys, Itys!*

from the ivy's dark,
the tangled leaves,
and climbs and soars,
> *Itys, Itys!*

till lord Apollo hears,
god with golden hair,
and sweeps his lovely lyre
in echo of your song,
> *Itys, Itys!*

and throats that cannot die
sing the sorrow back,
> *Itys! Itys! Itys!*

*There is a short coda by the flute, accompanied now by the distant sweeping of the lyre.*

**EUELPIDES**

Holy Zeus, just hear the little Birdie's song!
A sound like honey streaming through the woods . . .

**PISTHETAIROS**

Pssst.

Hush.

**EUELPIDES**

Hush? But why?

**PISTHETAIROS**

Shush.

**EUELPIDES**

But why?

**PISTHETAIROS**

The Hoopoe is preening to sing another song.

**HOOPOE**

*Singing, with flute obbligato.*

Epopopopopopopopopoi!
                    Popopopopopopopoi!
                        Io!  Io!  Io!
                Hear ye ye ye ye ye ye ye!

*Calling first to the landbirds.*

> O Birds of fellow feather come!
> Come, you Birds who graze, who feed
> over the farmers' fresh-sown fields!
> Barley-eating tribes, in thousands come!
> O peckers after seeds, hungry nations,
> swift of wing! Come, O chirrupers!
> All you who flitter in the furrows,
> who throng, who flock the new-turned sod,
> who sing your chirrup, chirrup-song,
>    *tio tio tio tio tio tio tio!*

> All you who in the gardens nest,
> who perch beneath the ivy's leaves!
> O rangers on the mountain, come,
> arbutus-stealers, olive-thieves!
> Flock, fly to my call! Come, O come!
>    *trio trio trio totobrix!*

*To the Birds of marsh and meadow.*

> O Birds of swamp and river, come!
> You whose beaks snap up the whining gnats,
> who splash in water where the earth is wet
> or skim the meadows over Marathon!
> O Birds of blazoned feather, come!

*To the Seabirds.*

> Come, Birds who soar upon the sea
> where the kingfisher swoops!
> O Birds with delicate necks,
> O taper-throated, come!
> Come and see the world remade!
> Come and see the Birds reborn!

> Lo, a MAN has come, of skill and craft,
>    whose wit cuts like a knife,
> and to the Birds he brings the Word
>    of more abundant life.

Hear ye, hear ye, hear ye!
Come to council, come!
Hither, hither, hither!

> *Toro toro toro tix*
> *kikka bau, kikka bau*
> *toro toro toro li*
>   *li lix!*

**PISTHETAIROS**

Hey, seen any Birds yet?

**EUELPIDES**

                Not a sign of one.
And my neck's damn near broken from looking too.

**PISTHETAIROS**

The way it looks to me, the Hoopoe hopped in
and whooped himself hoarse, and all for nothing.

**HOOPOE**

*Toro tix! Toro tix!*

*As the Hoopoe's call ends, the first member of the Chorus
enters. He is dressed as a Flamingo and is shortly followed by
other members, each costumed in broad representation of some
bird.*

**PISTHETAIROS**

Pssst. Euelpides! Look over there! There's a Bird coming in!

**EUELPIDES**

By Zeus, it *is* a Bird! What do you suppose he is? A
Peacock?

*Enter Hoopoe.*

**PISTHETAIROS**

The Hoopoe will tell us.
                —Say, what sort of Bird is that?

HOOPOE

That, my friend, is a rare marshbird. Not the sort of Bird you run into every day.

EUELPIDES

Golly, what a flaming red!

HOOPOE

Exactly. That Bird's a Flamingo.

EUELPIDES

Oooh. Look.

PISTHETAIROS

What is it?

EUELPIDES

That Bird.

*Enter a second bird, dressed in gorgeous Persian costume, with a magnificent strut.*

PISTHETAIROS

Say, he's exotic. Like something out of Aischylos.*
*Prithee, sir,*
*how is yon strange and mountain-ranging mantic Bird*
*yclept?*

HOOPOE

We call him the Bedouin Bird.

PISTHETAIROS

You don't say? The Bedouin Bird! But how could a Bedouin Bird get to Greece without a Camel Bird?

EUELPIDES

And look there! There comes another Bird with a whopping crest.

*Enter a Hoopoe.*

**PISTHETAIROS**

Say, that's odd. You mean you aren't the only Hoopoe
going? Is he a Hoopoe too?

**HOOPOE**

Yes indeed, he's a Hoopoe too.
But he's the son of the Hoopoe in Philokles' tragedy of
*Tereus.** I'm his grandpa, and he's my namesake,
Hoopoe Jr.—You know the pattern, the way Kallias calls
his son Hipponikos, and then these Hipponikoses call all
their sons Kalliases.

**EUELPIDES**

So this is the Kallias Hoopoe. Well, he sure looks plucked.

**HOOPOE**

He's quite the bird about town, so parasites strip him bare
and the chorus girls keep yanking his pretty feathers out.

*Enter a dazzlingly brilliant bird with an enormous crest and a
great protruding belly.*

**EUELPIDES**

Sweet Poseidon! Look at that gorgeous Birdic strutting in!
What's he called?

**HOOPOE**

That one? He's the Crested Guzzleguzzle.

**EUELPIDES**

The Guzzleguzzle, eh? I thought that was our boy
Kleonymos.*

**PISTHETAIROS**

No, this Bird has a crest. Our man is crestfallen now.
Don't you remember how he ditched his helmet and ran
away?

**EUELPIDES**

Look, Hoopoe, what's the point of all this crestwork on the Birds?* Dress parade?

**HOOPOE**

                    No. Partly self-defence, partly sanitation.
Some towns are built on crests of hills, others in the passes.
So some Birds sport their plumes on top, but others on
    their asses.

**PISTHETAIROS**

What an ungodly crowd of Birds! It gives me the jitters.

*The rest of the Chorus, birds of every size and description, now stream into the orchestra.*

Look, Birds everywhere!

**EUELPIDES**

                    Apollo, what a bevy of Birds!
Why, when they lift up their wings, they block out the
entrance.

**PISTHETAIROS**

Look, there's the Partridge!

**EUELPIDES**

                    And here's the Hooded Ptarmigan!

**PISTHETAIROS**

And there's a Widgeon, I think.

**EUELPIDES**

                    Here comes a female Plover.
But who's that Bird on her tail?

**PISTHETAIROS**

                    Her lover. The Horny Pecker.*

**EUELPIDES**

What does her husband say?

**PISTHETAIROS**

                        He's a queer Bird and doesn't care.

**HOOPOE**

Here's the Owl.

**PISTHETAIROS**

            Now there's a thought! Bringing Owls to Athens.*

**HOOPOE**

And Jay and Pigeon. Lark, Wren, Wheatear, and
Turtledove. Ringdove, Stockdove, Cuckoo, and Hawk.
Firecrest and Wren, Rail and Kestrel and Gull, Waxwing,
Woodpecker, and Vulture . . .

*In one last surge the remaining members of the Chorus stream
into the orchestra, ruffling their feathers and chirping and
hissing.*

**PISTHETAIROS**

Birds, Birds, billions of Birds!

**EUELPIDES**

*Indicating the Audience.*

                        But most of them Cuckoos and Geese.

**PISTHETAIROS**

What a skittering and cackling!

**EUELPIDES**

                        Unless I'm much mistaken,
I detect a note of menace.*

**PISTHETAIROS**

                        They *do* seem somewhat peeved.
You know, I think they're glaring at *us*.

**EUELPIDES**

Damn right they are.

**KORYPHAIOS**

Who-oo-chee-who-chee-who-oo-oo-oo
who-oo-chee-oo-oo has summoned me?

**HOOPOE**

Me, that's who. Your old friend Hoopoe.

**KORYPHAIOS**

Spea-pea-pea-pea-speak, Hoopopopopopoi.

**HOOPOE**

Listen. Great news! Glorious news!
News of Profit, gravy for all!
Two brilliant men have come to call
on me.

**KORYPHAIOS**

On YOU?
But HOW?
And WHO?

**HOOPOE**

But I'm trying to tell you.

Two old men have come to call,
two old refugees who have renounced the human race for
    good
and who bring us a glorious scheme, a Plan of fantastic
    proportions,
gigantic, sublime, colossal—

**KORYPHAIOS**

Colossal's the word for your blunder.
Have you lost your mind?

**HOOPOE**

Wait, listen . . .

KORYPHAIOS

Explain. And fast.

HOOPOE

Listen. I welcomed two old men. Harmless ornithologists,
infatuated with the Birds. They want to live with their
Feathered Friends.

KORYPHAIOS

What? You welcomed TWO MEN?

HOOPOE

What's more, I'd do it again.

KORYPHAIOS

You mean they're *here?* In our midst?

HOOPOE

As much as I. Look.

*He raises his wings, revealing the two men cowering behind
him.*

CHORUS

—O Treachery!
        O Treason!
                —O!
            BAD Hoopoe, to betray us so!
        To think that you, the Birdies' friend,
        could come to such a wicked end!
        To think that I should one day see
        the Bird who pecked the corn with me
                dishonor and disgrace
            the MAGNA CARTA of our race,
                and sell us to our foe!
—O Treachery!
        O Treason!
                —O!

**KORYPHAIOS**

All right, we'll settle accounts with this treacherous Hoopoe
later.
As for these venerable old fools, we'll settle with them right
now.
We'll shred them into tatters.

**PISTHETAIROS**

Gods, they're shredding us to tatters!

**EUELPIDES**

Well, it's all your fault. This whole damn trip was your idea.
Why in god's name did you lead me here?

**PISTHETAIROS**

To bring up my rear.

**EUELPIDES**

It's so hopeless I could cry.

**PISTHETAIROS**

Fat chance you'll have of crying.
Once those Birds are through with you, you won't have any
eyes.

**CHORUS**

Advance the wings and charge the flanks!
    The Rooster shrills ATTACK!
Aerial squadrons, take to the air!
    Beat your enemy back.

These men are spies, their lives are lies,
    so kill without regrets!
The skill to kill lies in your bills.
    Your beaks are bayonets.

No cloud exists, no breaker is,
    no fog on mountain peaks,
quite big or thick or black enough
    to save them from our beaks!

**KORYPHAIOS**

Mount the attack!
         Charge them, Birds! Bite them, tear them!
On the double!
         Captain on the right! Advance your wing and charge!

*The Chorus wheels in massed formation toward the stage. Euelpides in terror starts to run.*

**EUELPIDES**

They're charging! Where can we run?

**PISTHETAIROS**

         Run, man? Stand and fight!

**EUELPIDES**

And get torn to tatters?

**PISTHETAIROS**

         What good's running? *They*'re flying.

**EUELPIDES**

But what should I do?

**PISTHETAIROS**

         Listen to me and follow my orders.
First pick up that platter and use it as a shield. Now HOLD
THAT LINE!

**EUELPIDES**

But what good's a platter?

**PISTHETAIROS**

         Birds are skittish of platters.*
         They'll scatter.

**EUELPIDES**

Yeah? Well, what about that vulture there?

**PISTHETAIROS**

Snatch up a skewer.
Now stick it out front like a spear.

**EUELPIDES**

But what about my eyes?

**PISTHETAIROS**

Jam a jug on your head. Now cover your eyes with saucers.

**EUELPIDES**

What a kitchen tactician! What crockery-strategy! Gee,
old Nikias is tricky, but he can't compare with you.

**KORYPHAIOS**

FORWARD!
Spit them with your beaks! At 'em, Birds!
CHARGE!
Rip 'em, scratch 'em, flay 'em, bite! BUT BREAK THAT
POT!

**HOOPOE**

*Intervening.*

Truce, truce.
No more of this bitterness. You Birds should be
ashamed.
Why should you kill these men? What harm have they done
to you?
Somewhat more to the point, they're both closely related to
my wife.*

**KORYPHAIOS**

Why spare these men any more than wolves? What worse
enemy than men do we Birds have?

**HOOPOE**

Enemies by nature, I admit.
But these men are exceptions to the rule. They come to you
as friends.

Moreover, they bring a scheme from which we Birds stand
  to profit.

**KORYPHAIOS**

Are you suggesting that Birds should take advice from men?
What can *we* learn from men?

**HOOPOE**

           If wise men learn from their enemies,
  then why not you?
        Remember the advantage of keeping
          an open mind.
Preparedness, after all, is not a lesson taught us by our
  friends
but by our enemies. It is our enemies, not our friends, who
  teach us to survive.
I might cite the case of cities: was it from their friends or
  their foes
that mankind first learned to build walls and ships in self-
  defence?
But that one lesson still preserves us all and all we have.

**KORYPHAIOS**

There's something in what you say.
            Perhaps we'd better hear them.

**PISTHETAIROS**

*To Euelpides.*

They're beginning to show signs of reason. Don't say a word.

**HOOPOE**

*To the Chorus.*

That's better, friends. You're doing right, and you'll thank
  me for it later.

**KORYPHAIOS**

We've never disobeyed your advice before.

PISTHETAIROS

They seem more
peaceful now.

So you can ground the pan
and put the platter down.
But stand your ground
and keep that spit on hand,
while I look round
our little camp of crocks
and see how matters stand
by peeking over pots.

EUELPIDES

Chief, suppose we die
in combat?

PISTHETAIROS

Then we'll lie
in Athens at public cost.*
They'll give us hero's honors
and bury us like gods
when we say our lives were lost
fighting foreign soldiers
at very heavy odds.
In fact, I'll use those very words
(omitting, for effect, of course
any reference to Birds.)*

KORYPHAIOS

All right, you Birds, FALL IN!
The war's over.
                AT EASE!
You there, quiet!
                QUIET, PLEASE!

*The Chorus returns to its normal position in the orchestra.
Much whispering, nodding, and shuffling. Then silence.*

Now we have to inquire
who these strangers are
and why they've come.
Look here, Hoopoe.

HOOPOE

Um?

KORYPHAIOS

Who are these fellows?

HOOPOE

Two humans from Hellas
where genius grows greener than grass.

KORYPHAIOS

But why have they come?
What do they hope to get from the Birds?

HOOPOE

Their motive is Love.
Love is the burden of all their words.
Love of your life
and Love of you,
to live with you
in Love always.

KORYPHAIOS

Is *that* what they say?
But what is the gist of their scheme?

HOOPOE

They envisage a vision of glory,
a dream so fantastic
it staggers the sensible mind.

KORYPHAIOS

Well, it doesn't stagger mine.
What's in it for them?
Who are they trying to stick?

HOOPOE

No one.
This is no trick.

What this means is bliss.
Believe me, utter bliss. Sheer
and absolute.
            *Viz.*
all shall be yours,
whatever is,
here or there,
far or near,
all, everywhere.
And this they swear.

*[handwritten margin note: thru parodial to power]*

**KORYPHAIOS**

Crackpots, eh?

**HOOPOE**

Right as rain.
Foxes, not men.
Boxes of slyness,
brimming with brain.

**KORYPHAIOS**

Then let them talk! We're all in a twitter to hear.

**HOOPOE**

So be it, then.
            —Men, take these weapons inside
the house and hang them up beside the blazing hearth
where the god of fire presides. They'll bring us luck.

*Servants pick up the pots and plates and skewers and carry
them inside. The Hoopoe turns to Pisthetairos.*

Pisthetairos, you have the floor. Proceed with your case.
Explain your proposal.

**PISTHETAIROS**

            By Apollo, only on condition
that you Birds agree to swear a solemn truce with me
like the truce which that armor-making baboon—you know
    who I mean—*
signed with his wife: no biting, scratching, or cutting,
no hauling around by the balls, no shoving things—

**EUELPIDES**

*Bending over.*

—Up there?

**PISTHETAIROS**

In my eyes, I was going to say.

**KORYPHAIOS**

We accept your terms.

**PISTHETAIROS**

First you have to swear to them.

**KORYPHAIOS**

We swear it then, but on this one condition only:
that you guarantee that this comedy of ours will win First
Prize by completely unanimous vote of the Judges.

**PISTHETAIROS**

Agreed.

**KORYPHAIOS**

Splendid. If, however, we Birds should break the truce,
we agree to forfeit, say, forty-nine per cent
of the votes.

**HOOPOE**

*To the Chorus.*

Fall out!

Pick up your weapons, men
and return at once to your quarters. On the double!
Company Assignments will be posted on the bulletin boards.

**CHORUS**

—Man by nature is a liar made.
He plays a double game.

—Dishonesty's his stock-in-trade.
Deception is his name.
—We say no more.
                    —But it may be
your canny mortal brain may see
what our poor feeble wits cannot—
—some gift of noble intellect
we once possessed and then forgot
as our race declined;
—some genius of the will
or wisdom of the mind,
—grown rusty with neglect,
but fusting in us still.
—It seems to us fantastic.
—But still, it *could* be true.
—And, of course, we'd split the profits—
—if any such accrue.

**KORYPHAIOS**

Pisthetairos, proceed. You may say whatever you wish. With
    impunity.
We pledge you our words as Birds: we won't renege on the
    truce.

**PISTHETAIROS**

By god, I'm wild to begin!
                    The dough of my vision has risen,
and there's nothing now but the kneading.
                    —Boy, bring me a wreath.
Someone fetch water for my hands.*

**EUELPIDES**

                                    Hey, we going to a feast?

**PISTHETAIROS**

A dinner of words, a fat and succulent haunch of speech,
a meal to shiver the soul.
                    —Unhappy Birds, I grieve for you,
you who once were kings—

**KORYPHAIOS**

—Kings? Of what?

**PISTHETAIROS**

Kings of everything.
Kings of creation. My kings. This man's kings. Kings of
    king Zeus.
More ancient than Kronos. Older than Titans. Older than
    Earth.

**KORYPHAIOS**

*Older than Earth?*

**PISTHETAIROS**

Older than Earth.

**KORYPHAIOS**

And to think I never suspected!

**PISTHETAIROS**

Because you're a lazy Bird* and you haven't reread your
    Aesop.
For Aesop states that the Lark is the oldest thing in the
    world,
older than Earth. So ancient, in fact, that when her father
    died,
she couldn't find him a grave, for the Earth hadn't yet been
    made,
and therefore couldn't be dug. So what on earth could she
    do?
Well, the little Lark was stumped. Then suddenly she had it!
She laid her daddy out and buried him under her tail.

**EUELPIDES**

She did for a fact.
And that's how Asbury* got its name.

**PISTHETAIROS**

Hence my argument stands thus: if the Birds are older than
    Earth,
and therefore older than gods, then the Birds are the heirs
    of the world.
For the oldest always inherits.

**EUELPIDES**

                        It stands to reason, friends.
So pack some bone in your bills and hone them down to
    a point.
Old Zeus won't rush to resign and let the Woodpeckers
    reign.*

**PISTHETAIROS**

Think of it, the springtime of the world!
                        The Age of the Birds!
Primal lords of Creation! Absolute masters of man!
But the gods are mere upstarts and usurpers of very recent
    date.
And proof abounds.
                    Let me adduce, for instance, the case of
                        the Rooster.
Aeons and aeons ago, ages before the age of Darius,
the kingdom of Persia lay prostrate beneath the sway of the
    Rooster
And the Rooster, ever since, has been called the Persian Red.

**EUELPIDES**

And that's why, even now, he swaggers and struts like a
    king
and keeps a harem of hens. And, unique among the Birds,
he wears the royal red tiara of the ancient Persian kings.

**PISTHETAIROS**

And talk of power!
                    Why, even now its memory remains,
enshrined in habit. For when the Cock his matins crows,
mankind goes meekly off to work—bakers, smiths, and
    potters,

tanners and merchants and musical-instrument makers.
And when he crows at dusk, the night-shift goes.

**EUELPIDES**

I'll vouch for that.
It was thanks to his night-shift crowing that I lost my
warmest coat.
I'd gone downtown to dinner, see, in honor of a birth.
Well, after a while I'd had five or six and passed out cold,
when that blasted Rooster started to crow. Needless to say,
I thought it was dawn, jumped into my clothes and tore off
to work.
But just outside the gate, somebody conked me with a club
and I passed out cold again. And when I came to, no coat!

**PISTHETAIROS**

What's more, once upon a time the Kites were the kings of
Hellas.

**KORYPHAIOS**

The *kings* of Hellas?

**PISTHETAIROS**

Right. The Kites were the kings of Hellas.
And it was during their reign that the custom begar in
Greece
of falling flat on your face whenever you saw a Kite.*

**EUELPIDES**

You know, I once spotted a Kite and went down on the
ground—
so damn hard I swallowed my money* and two of my teeth.
I damn near starved.

**PISTHETAIROS**

And once the Cuckoo was king of Egypt.

And when the call of the Cuckoo was heard in the land,
  every Egyptian
grabbed his scythe and ran to the fields to reap.

**EUELPIDES**

That's a fact.
And that's why, even today, we still call the Egyptians
cuckoo.*

**PISTHETAIROS**

Why, so great was the power of the Birds that even the
  greatest kings—
Agamemnon and Menelaos, to name only two of the
  greatest—
had their sceptres tipped with Birds, and the Birds got a cut
  in the take.

**EUELPIDES**

So *that's* it. That explains all that funny business in the plays
. I never understood before—where Priam, for instance,
  walks in,
and there on his sceptre, large as life, some Bird is perching.
I used to think he was there to keep an eye peeled down
  below
on the rows where the politicians sit,* to see where our
  money goes.            *attacking politicians*

**PISTHETAIROS**

But the crowning proof is this: the present incumbent, Zeus,
wears an Eagle upon his helmet as the symbol of royal
  power.
Athena uses the Owl, and Apollo, as aide to Zeus, a Hawk.

**EUELPIDES**

By Demeter, they do! But why do the gods use these Birds
as emblems?

**PISTHETAIROS**

An unconscious admission of the Birds' ancient power and
  supremacy.

That's why when men sacrifice to the gods, the Birds swoop
   down and snatch the food,
thereby beating out the gods, and so asserting their old
   priority.
Again, no one ever swore by the gods, but always by the
   Birds.

EUELPIDES

Doctors still swear by the Duck.* That's why we call them
   quacks.

PISTHETAIROS

But these were the honors you held in the days of your
greatness.

        Whereas now you've been downgraded.
        You're the slaves, not lords, of men.
        They call you brainless or crazy.
        They kill you whenever they can.

        The temples are no protection:
        the hunters are lying in wait
        with traps and nooses and nets
        and little limed twigs and bait.

        And when you're taken, they sell you
        as tiny *hors d'oeuvres* for a lunch.
        And you're not even sold alone,
        but lumped and bought by the bunch.

        And buyers come crowding around
        and pinch your breast and your rump,
        to see if your fleshes are firm
        and your little bodies are plump.

        Then, as if this weren't enough,
        they refuse to roast you whole,
        but dump you down in a dish
        and call you a *casserôle*.

        They grind up cheese and spices
        with some oil and other goo,

and they take this slimy gravy
and they pour it over you!

*Yes, they pour it over you!*

It's like a disinfectant,
and they pour it piping hot,
as though your meat were putrid,
to sterilize the rot!

*Yes, to sterilize the rot!*

*As Pisthetairos finishes, a long low susurrus of grief runs
through the Chorus and the Birds sigh, weep, and beat their
breasts with their wings.*

CHORUS

Stranger, forgive us if we cry,
    reliving in your words
those years of cowardice that brought
    disaster to the Birds:—
    that tragic blunder
    and our fathers' crime,
    complacency whose cost
    was greatness and our name,
    as dignity went under
    in a chicken-hearted time,
    and all was lost.

But now, by luck,
or heaven-sent,
a Man has come
to pluck us from disgrace.

Hail, Pisthetairos!
Hail, Savior of the Birds,
Redeemer of our Race!
To you we now commit:
        ourselves,
        our nests,
        our chicks,
            *et cet.*

**KORYPHAIOS**

Sir, you have the floor once more. Proceed with your
explanation. Until our power is restored, life means less
than nothing to the Birds.

**PISTHETAIROS**

My Plan, in gist, is this—a city of the Birds,
whose walls and ramparts shall include the atmosphere of
   the world
within their circuit. But make the walls of brick, like
   Babylon.

**EUELPIDES**

A Babylon of the Birds!* What a whopping, jumbo-size city!

**PISTHETAIROS**

The instant your walls are built, reclaim your sceptre from
   Zeus.
If he shilly-shallies or fobs you off with a lot of excuses,
proclaim a Holy War, a Great Crusade against the gods.
Then slap embargoes on their lust, forbidding any gods
in manifest state of erection to travel through your sky
on amatory errands down to Earth to lay their women—
their Semeles, Alkmenes, and so forth. Then, if they attempt
   to ignore
your warning, place their offending peckers under bond
as contraband and seal them shut. That will stop their fun,
I think.
      Second, appoint some Bird as your official ambassador
to men, and serve them formal notice that the Birds demand
   priority
in all their sacrifices. The leftovers, of course, will go to the
   gods.
But for the future, even when they offer sacrifices to the
   gods,
each Bird must be paired with a god*—whichever one seems
   most apt.
Thus, if Aphrodite is offered a cake, the Wagtail will get one
   too.

When Poseidon gets his sheep, the Seagull must have his
    wheat.
Greedy Herakles shall eat—when the glutton Jay is fed.
And as for Zeus, why, Zeus must wait his turn until the
    Kinglet,
lord of all the Birds, receives his sacrificial gnat.

EUELPIDES

I *like* that gnat. Old has-been Zeus can rumble with rage!

KORYPHAIOS

But why should men believe we're gods and not just shabby
Birds? These wings are a giveaway.

PISTHETAIROS

                    Rubbish. Hermes is a god, isn't he?
But he goes flapping around on wings. And so do loads of
    gods.
There's Victory on "gildered wings," and don't forget the
    god of Love.
And Homer says that Iris looks like a dove with the jitters.

EUELPIDES

And lightning too, that's got wings. Hey, what if lightning
fell on us?

KORYPHAIOS

And what if men are blind and go on truckling to Olympos
and refuse to worship the Birds?

PISTHETAIROS

                    Then swarms of starving Sparrows
shall descend on their fields in millions and gobble up their
    seeds.
They'll damn well go hungry. We'll see then if Demeter will
    feed them.

EUELPIDES

If I know that Demeter, she'll have plenty of excuses ready.

PISTHETAIROS

Then we'll muster the Crows and Ravens and send them
  down in droves
to peck out the eyes of the oxen and make the sheep go
  blind.
Dr. Apollo can cure them—but I'd hate to pay the fee.

EUELPIDES

Give me the nod when you're ready. I want to unload my
ox.

PISTHETAIROS

If, on the other hand, mankind accepts you as their gods,
their manifest Poseidon, their Earth, their Principle of Life,
all their wishes shall come true.

KORYPHAIOS

                           All their wishes? For instance?

PISTHETAIROS     *argument in favor of bird rule*

Why, enormous plagues of locusts will not infest their vines:
a single regiment of our Owls will wipe the locusts out.
And the gallfly and the mite will no longer blight their figs
since we'll send down troops of Thrushes to annihilate the
  bugs.

KORYPHAIOS

But what about money? Money's Man's dominant passion.

PISTHETAIROS

Duck soup for you. Your oracles will tell them what they
want—the whereabouts of the richest mines, when the

market is right to make a killing, and so forth. And no more shipwrecks either.

**KORYPHAIOS**

No more shipwrecks?

**PISTHETAIROS**

No shipwrecks. You take your omens, you see, and some Bird pipes up, "Bad weather brewing" or "Forecast: fair."

**EUELPIDES**

To hell with the Birds! A ship for me! I'm off to sea!

**PISTHETAIROS**

You'll show them buried treasure; you'll tell them where to find gold.
For Birds know all the answers, or so the saying goes—
"A little Bird told me." People are always saying that.

**EUELPIDES**

The hell with the sea! A shovel for me! I'm off to dig for gold!

**KORYPHAIOS**

But how will we give them health? That lies in the hands of the gods.

**PISTHETAIROS**

Give them wealth, you give them health. They're really much the same.

**EUELPIDES**

And that's a fact. The man who's sick is always doing badly.

**KORYPHAIOS**

But longevity and old age also lie in the hands of the gods.

How will a man grow old if the gods refuse him Old Age?
Will he die in childhood?

**PISTHETAIROS**

Die? The Birds will add to his life
three centuries at least.

**KORYPHAIOS**

But how?

**PISTHETAIROS**

From their own lives, of course.
What doth the poet say?
"Five lives of men the cawing Crow
outliveth."*

**EUELPIDES**

Long live the Birds! Down with Zeus!

**PISTHETAIROS**

I'm with you there,
and think of the money we'll save!

For Birds won't want any shrines;
    marble just leaves them cold.
They don't give a hoot for temples
    with doors of beaten gold.

They'll live in woodses and copses—
    that's plenty of shrine for them.
And the social-register swells
    can strut on an olive limb.*

And we'll go no more to Delphi!
    To hell with Ammon's seat!
We'll amble out under the olives
    and toss them bits of wheat,

and hold up our paws to heaven
    and make the Birds a prayer,

> and the Birds will grant all our wishes
>     for cutting them a share.
>
> And we won't be out of pocket.
>     No, the only dough we'll need
> is a little loaf of barley
>     and a tiny pinch of seed.

**KORYPHAIOS**

The Birds' best friend! And to think how we misjudged you
once, most generous of men!
                        Ask us what you will. It shall be done.

**CHORUS**

*Amen*, we say.
                    And now, presuming you concur,
                        we Birds propose an oath
                    of mutual assistance, sir,
                        and binding on us both.

> Arm to wing, we'll soar to war!
>     Our cause needs no excuse.
> We'll storm up Mt. Olympos, friend,
>     and make a pulp of Zeus!

**KORYPHAIOS**

We await your orders, sir. Tasks that need mere brawn and
    muscle
we Birds can do. The complicated mental stuff we leave to
    you.

**HOOPOE**

Action, dammit, action! That's what we need.
Strike while the iron's hot. No dawdling around
like slowpoke Nikias.
                    —Dear me, I nearly forgot.
You two gentlemen must see my little nest,
my trash of sticks and straw and kickshaw stuff.
And good heavens! We haven't been formally introduced.

**PISTHETAIROS**

Pisthetairos here.

**HOOPOE**

Ah. And this gentleman?

**EUELPIDES**

Euelpides.

From Athens.

**HOOPOE**

Enchanted, I'm sure.

**PISTHETAIROS**

The pleasure's ours.

**HOOPOE**

Please come in.

**PISTHETAIROS**

No, after you.

**HOOPOE**

This way, gentlemen.

*The Hoopoe begins to flap his wings to flutter into his nest.*

**PISTHETAIROS**

Hey, you!
Damn it, stop! Back water, blast you!
Look here, what sort of partnership is this supposed to be
if you start taking off when we can't even fly?

**HOOPOE**

Does it matter?

**PISTHETAIROS**

Remember what old Aesop tells us*

in his fable of the Eagle and the Fox in business
who couldn't get along? The Fox got swindled by the Eagle.

HOOPOE

Don't be nervous. I know of a wonderful magic root.
Merely nibble on it and you'll sprout a set of wings.

PISTHETAIROS

Splendid. Then let's go in.
                              —You there, Xanthias.
Hey, Manodorus! Bring our luggage inside the house.

KORYPHAIOS

One moment, please, Hoopoe, when you go inside . . .

HOOPOE

                                                    Yes?

KORYPHAIOS

By all means take your human guests and feast them well.
But first do one little favor for the Chorus, please.
Bring out your wife, your lovely Nightingale,
the bird with honeyed tongue, the Muses' love,
and let the Chorus play with her a little while.

PISTHETAIROS

I add my entreaty to theirs. In the name of heaven,
bring her out from the bed of rushes where she hides.

EUELPIDES

*Please, please do.* Bring the pretty Birdie out.
I've never met a Nightingale before.

HOOPOE

                                        With all my heart.
I'd be delighted, gentlemen.

*Calling inside.*

                    Oh Prokne! Prokne.
Please come out, my dear, and meet our visitors.

*A lovely well-rounded young flutegirl shyly appears. She is dressed in the rich gold-encrusted robes of a young Athenian matron of high birth. On her head she wears the mask of the Nightingale.*

PISTHETAIROS

Almighty Zeus! Gosh, what a baby of a Birdie!
What curves! What grace! What a looker!

EUELPIDES

                            Gee! By god,
I'd like to bounce between her thighs right now!

                            " low " *censor*

PISTHETAIROS

And what a shimmer of gold! Just like a bride.

EUELPIDES

By god, I've got half a mind to kiss her!

PISTHETAIROS

                            Look out,
you old lecher, her beak's a pair of skewers.

EUELPIDES

                            Very well.
Then I'll treat her like an egg and peel her shell.
I'll lift her little mask and kiss her—so.

HOOPOE

Harrumph. This way.

PISTHETAIROS

                    And may good fortune go with us.

*Exeunt Pisthetairos, Euelpides, and Hoopoe, followed by the slaves with the luggage.*

CHORUS

> O love,
>            tawnythroat!
> Sweet nightingale,
> musician of the Birds
> Come and sing,
>           honey-throated one!
> Come, O love,
>           flutist of the Spring,
> accompany our song.

*The Chorus turns sharply and faces the audience,\* while the
flutegirl begins the song of the nightingale at its most mournful.
The flute obbligato accompanies the Chorus throughout.*

O suffering mankind,
             lives of twilight,
                         race feeble and fleeting,
like the leaves scattered!
                   Pale generations,
                               creatures of clay,
the wingless, the fading!
                   Unhappy mortals,
                               shadows in time,
flickering dreams!
             Hear us now,
                   the ever-living Birds,
the undying,
       the ageless ones,
                   scholars of eternity.
Hear and learn from us
             the truth
                   of all there is to know—
what we are,
       and how the gods began,
                   of Chaos and Dark.
(And when you know
             tell Prodikos to go
                         hang:\* he's had it!)
There was Chaos at first
             and Night and Space
                         and Tartaros.
There was no Earth.

No Heaven was.
But sable-wingèd Night
laid her wind-egg there*
in the boundless lap
of infinite Dark.
And from that egg,
in the seasons' revolving,
Love was born,
the graceful, the golden,
the whirlwind Love
on gleaming wings.
And there in the waste
of Tartaros,
Love with Chaos lay
and hatched the Birds.
We come from Love.
Love brought us
to the light.
There were no gods
till Love had married
all the world in love.
Then the world was made.
Blue Heaven stirred,
and Ocean,
the Earth and ageless gods,
the blessèd ones
who do not die.
But we came first.
We Birds were born
the first-born sons of
Love,
in proof whereof
we wear Love's wings,
we help his lovers.
How many pretty boys,
their prime not past,
abjuring Love,
have opened up their thighs
and yielded,
overborne by us,
bribed by a Bird,
a Coot, a Goose,
a little Persian Cock!

Think of the services
            we Birds perform
                        for all mankind.
We mark your seasons off,
                summer, spring,
                        winter, fall.
When for Africa
        the screaming Crane departs,
                        you sow your fields.
And then the sailor
            takes his ease
                    and hangs his rudder up,
and thief Orestes
        weaves himself a cloak
                        and robs no man.
And then the Kite appears,
                whose coming says
                        the Spring is here,
the time has come
            to shear the sheep.
                        And so the Swallow
brings his summer,
            when mankind lays
                    its winter weeds away.
And we are Ammon
            and Dodona.
                    We are your Apollo,
that prophetic voice
            to whom you turn
                    in everything you do—
practical affairs,
            commerce and trade,
                    and marriage too.
Birds are your signs,
            and all your omens
                    are governed by Birds:
words are omens
        sent by the Birds.
                    And the same for sneezes,
meetings, asses, voices:
            all are omens,
                    and omens are Birds.

Who are we then
        if we are not
                your prophetic Apollo?

*The obbligato of the flute ceases as the Chorus now shifts to a lighter vein and a quicker tempo.*

So elect us as your gods
and we, in turn, shall be
your weathervane and Muse,
your priests of prophecy,
    foretelling all,
winter, summer, spring, and fall.

Furthermore, we promise we'll
give mankind an honest deal.
Unlike our smug opponent, Zeus,
we'll stop corruption and abuse.
NO ABSENTEE ADMINISTRATION!
NO PERMANENT VACATION
IN THE CLOUDS!
                And we promise
to be scrupulously honest.

Last of all, we guarantee
to every single soul on earth,
his sons and their posterity:
        HEALTH
        WEALTH
        HAPPINESS
        YOUTH
        LONG LIFE
        LAUGHTER
        PEACE
        DANCING
          and
        LOTS TO EAT!
We'll mince no words.
Your lives shall be
the milk of the Birds!
We guarantee
you'll all be
revoltingly
RICH!

O woodland Muse
with lovely throat,
*tio tio tio tinx!*
who with me sing
whenas in glade or mountain, I,
perched upon the ashtree cry,
*tio tio tio tinx!*
my tawny-throated song of praise,
to cal! the Mother to the dance,
a song of joy for blessed Pan,
*totototototinx!*
whence, like a bee,
the poet stole his honeyed song,*
my ravished cry,
*tio tio tio tinx!*


Do *you* suffer pangs of conscience?

Nervous?

Jumpy?

Scared?

Need a hideout from the law? Some cozy place to pass the
time? Well, step right up, friend!

We'll get you a berth with the Birds.
We do things differently up here.

What your laws condemn,
the things that you think shady or immoral are compulsory
with us.
Consider the case, for instance, of a boy who beats up his
dad.
Admit it: you're shocked. The idea! But *we* call it courage
when some bantam twirps, "C'mon, old Bird, put up your
spurs and fight!"
Or suppose you've deserted. You're a runaway, branded
with shame.
Hell, come and live with us! We'll call you a Yellow
Chicken.
Or perhaps you happen to come from some foppish hole in
Asia?
Come on up, you fairy fop, and be an Asiatic Finch.
Or suppose you're a slave from Krete, like our friend
Exekestides—
We'll call you little Cuckoo and pawn you off as our own.

Was Peisias your father?

Are you a future traitor too?

Hell, make like a Partridge then. That's what your Daddy did.

And who are we Birds to fuss at shamming hurt and
partridge tricks?

And so the swans
their clamor cry,
*tio tio tio tinx!*
and beating wings
and bursting throats
lord Apollo sing,
*tio tio tio tinx!*

by Hebros' waters, swarming, crying,
*tio tio tio tinx!*
And every living thing is still.
On bird, on beast, the hush of awe.
The windless sea lies stunned when—
*totototototinx!*
All Olympos rings,
and wonder breaks upon the gods,
and echoing, the Graces sing,
and lovely Muses raise the cry,
*tio tio tio tinx!*

Friends, you haven't really lived till you've tried a set of
FEATHERS!

Think, spectators.

Imagine yourselves with a pair of wings!
The sheer joy of it! Not having to sit those tragedies out!
No getting bored. You merely flap your little wings and fly
off home.
You have a snack, then make it back to catch the COMIC
play.
Or again, suppose you're overtaken by a sudden need to crap.
Do you do it in your pants?

Not a bit.

You just zoom off,
fart and shit to your heart's content and whizz right back.
Or perhaps you're having an affair—I won't name any names.
You spot the lady's husband attending some meeting or
other.

Up you soar, flap your wings, through the window and into
  bed!
You make it a quickie, of course, then flutter back to your
  seat.
So what do you say?
                    Aren't wings just the most *wonderful* things?
Look at Dieitrephes, our vulgar Ikaros of trade,*
who started life on wicker wings but rose to captain's rank,
and now, still riding high, is colonel of a wing of horse.
From horse's ass to Pegasos! But *that's* what wings can do!

*end sales pitch*

*The Chorus now turns and faces the stage as Pisthetairos and
Euelpides return. Both of them now sport tiny wings, a few
feathers, and outsize beaks.*

PISTHETAIROS

Well, here we are.

EUELPIDES

                    Sweet gods, in all my days,
I've never seen a sillier sight than you!

PISTHETAIROS

                                        Yeah,
what's so damn funny?

EUELPIDES

                    You and those baby wings.
They tickle me. You know what you look like, don't you?

PISTHETAIROS

*You* look like an abstraction of a Goose.

EUELPIDES

                                    Yeah?
Well, if you're supposed to be a Blackbird, boy,
somebody botched the job. You're more bare than Bird.

PISTHETAIROS

We made the choice that gave these barbs their bite.

Remember the poor Birds in that Aischylos play*—
"Shot down by shafts of their own feathers made?"

EUELPIDES

What's the next move?

PISTHETAIROS

First, we'll give our city
some highfalutin' name. Then a special sacrifice
to our new gods.

EUELPIDES

A special sacrifice? Yummy.

KORYPHAIOS

To work, men. How do you propose to name our city?

PISTHETAIROS

How about Sparta? That's a grand old name
with a fine pretentious ring.

EUELPIDES

Great Herakles,
call my city Sparta? I wouldn't even insult
my mattress by giving it a name like Sparta.*

PISTHETAIROS

Well,
what do you suggest instead?

FUELPIDES

Something big, smacking
of the clouds. A pinch of fluff and rare air.
A swollen sound.

PISTHETAIROS

I've got it! Listen—
CLOUDCUCKOOLAND!

**KORYPHAIOS**

That's it! The perfect name. And it's a *big* word too.

**EUELPIDES**

CLOUDCUCKOOLAND!
                       Imagination's happy home,
where Theogenes builds castles in the air, and Aischines
becomes a millionaire.

**PISTHETAIROS**

                  Better yet, here we have
the plain of Phlegra, that windy battlefield of blah and bluff,
where the gabbling gods outbragged the wordy giants.

**KORYPHAIOS**

A suave and splendid city.
                    —But which of the gods
should we designate as patron and protector?

**EUELPIDES**

                            Why not Athena?

**PISTHETAIROS**

But it's bound to seem a bit odd, isn't it? I mean,
a female goddess protecting our walls with a spear
while men like Kleisthenes sit home with their knitting?

**KORYPHAIOS**

And, come to think of it, who will guard our Storkade?*

**PISTHETAIROS**

A Bird.

**KORYPHAIOS**

       One of us, you mean?

**PISTHETAIROS**

                     Why not the Rooster?

They're terrible scrappers and famous fighting Birds.
Little chicks of Ares.

**EUELPIDES**

        Little Corporal Cock!
He's the perfect Bird for protecting our rock.

**PISTHETAIROS**

*To Euelpides.*

Hop it, man!*
        Quick, up the rigging of the air!
Hurry! Done? Now supervise the workers on the wall.
Run the rubble up!
        Quick, mix the mortar, man!
Up the ladder with your hod—and then fall down!
Don't stop!
      Post the sentries!
             Bank the furnace!
Now the watchman's round.
               All right, catch two winks.
Rise and shine!
       Now send your heralds off,
one to the gods above, one to the mortals below.
Then scurry back.

**EUELPIDES**

        As for you, just stay right here—
and I hope you choke.

**PISTHETAIROS**

        Obey your orders, friend.
Unless you do your share, we shan't get done.

*Exit Euelpides.*

Now, let me see.
        First, a priest to supervise
our sacrifice.
       —Boy!

*An Acolyte appears.*

      Boy, go fetch me a priest.

And when you're finished, bring me a basket and a laver.

*Exit Acolyte.*

CHORUS

> The Birds agree
> most heartily.
>     You're absolutely right.
>
> Hymns and laud
> are dear to god,
>     but dinner's their delight.
>
> Yes, gratitude
> is shown with food,
>     so rise and offer up,
>
> in witness of
> our shrunken love,
>     one miserable lamp chop!

KORYPHAIOS

> Flutist, come in.*
> Now let our sacrifice begin.

*Enter the Flutist, a Raven whose beak is an enormous flute which is strapped to his mouth by means of a leather harness. After strenuous huffing, he manages to produce what are unmistakably caws.*

PISTHETAIROS

Stop that raucous Rook!
                In the name of god,
what are you anyway?
                I've seen some weird sights,
but this is the first time in my life I ever saw
a Blackbird propping his beak with a leather belt.*

*Exit Flutist. Enter Priest, followed by the Acolyte with the paraphernalia of the sacrifice.*

At last.
        —Eminence, you may begin the inaugural sacrifice.

PRIEST

Your humble servant, sir.

        —But where's my acolyte?

*The Acolyte steps forward. The Priest raises his hands and begins the Bidding Prayer of the Birds.\**

Now let us pray—
   PRAY TO THE HESTIA OF NESTS,
   TO THE HOUSEHOLDING HARRIER HAWK,
   TO ALL THE OLYMPIAN COCKS AND
     COQUETTES,
   TO THE SWOOPING STORK OF THE SEA—

PISTHETAIROS

ALL HAIL, THE STORK! HAIL, POSEIDON OF
  PINIONS!

PRIEST

   TO THE SWEETSINGER OF DELOS,
   THE APOLLONIAN SWAN,
   TO LETO THE QUEEN OF THE QUAIL,
   TO ARTEMIS THE PHOEBE—

PISTHETAIROS

HAIL TO THE PHOEBE, VIRGIN SISTER OF
  PHOIBOS!

PRIEST

   PRAY TO WOODPECKER PAN,
   TO DOWITCHER KYBELE,
   MOTHER OF MORTALS AND GODS—

PISTHETAIROS

HAIL, DOWAGER QUEEN, GREAT MOTHER OF
  BUSTARDS!

PRIEST

   PRAY THAT THEY GRANT US
   HEALTH AND LENGTH OF LIFE,

PRAY THAT THEY PROTECT US,
pray for the Chians too*—

PISTHETAIROS

You know, I like the way he tacks those Chians on.

PRIEST

COME, ALL HERO BIRDS,
ALL HEROINE HENS AND PULLETS!
COME, O GALLINULE!
BRING DICKYBIRD AND DUNNOCK,
COME, CROSSBILL AND BUNTING!
ON DIPPER, ON DIVER,
ON WHIMBREL AND FINCH!
COME CURLEW AND CREEPER,
ON PIPIT, ON PARROT,
COME VULTURE, COME TIT—

PISTHETAIROS

Stop it, you fool! Stop that rollcall of the Birds!
Are you utterly daft, man, inviting Vultures and Eagles
and suchlike to our feast? Or weren't you aware
one single beak could tuck it all away?
Clear out, and take your blasted ribands with you.
So help me, I'll finish this sacrifice myself.

*Exit Priest.*

CHORUS   *[handwritten: making fun of sacrificial rites]*

Again we raise
the hymn of praise
    and pour the sacred wine.

With solemn rite
we now invite
    the blessed gods to dine.

But don't *all* come—
perhaps just one,
    and maybe then again,

there's not enough
(besides, it's tough),
so stay away. Amen.

**PISTHETAIROS**

Let us pray to the pinion'd gods—

*Enter a hungry, ragged Poet, chanting.*

**POET**

In all thy songs, O Muse,
let one city
praisèd be—
CLOUDCUCKOOLAND THE LOVELY!

**PISTHETAIROS**

Who spawned this spook?
——Look here, who are you?

**POET**

One of the tribe of dulcet tongue and tripping speech—
"the slave of Poesy,
whose ardent soul
the Muses hold in thrall,"
as Homer hath it.*

**PISTHETAIROS**

Judging from your clothes, friend, your Muses must be
bankrupt. Tell me, bard, what ill wind plopped you here?

**POET**

I've been composing poems in honor of your new city—
oodles of little odes, some dedication-anthems,
songs for soprano voice, a lyric or two
*à la Simonides*—

**PISTHETAIROS**

How long has your little poetic mill
been grinding out this chaff?

POET

>              Why, simply ages.
> Long, long since my Muse commenced to sing
> Cloudcuckooland in all her orisons.

PISTHETAIROS

>                              Long ago?
> But that's impossible. This city's still a baby.
> I just now gave birth. I just baptised her.

POET

> *Ah, but swift are the mouths of the Muses,*
> *more swift than steeds the galloping news*
> *of the Muses!*

*He turns to the altar and with outstretched hands invokes it in Pindaric parody.*

>              O Father,
>                    Founder of Etna,*
>              of thy bounty give,
>              O Hiero, O Homonym,
>              Great Hero of the Fire,
>              just one slender sliv-
>              -er to my desire,
>              some tidbit to savor,
>              some token of favor—

PISTHETAIROS

> You know, I think we'd better bribe this beggar bard
> to leave before we die of doggerel.

*To the Acolyte.*

>                        —You there,
> strip and let the beggar poet have your overcoat.

*He hands the coat to the Poet.*

Dress.

>         Why, you poor poet, you're shivering with cold.

POET

> My Muse accepts with thanks
> this modest donation.
>
> But first, before I leave,
> one brief quotation,
> a snatch of Pindar
> you might ponder—

PISTHETAIROS

Gods above, will this poor man's Pindar never leave?

POET

> *Undressed amidst the nomad Skyths,\**
> *the Frozen Poet fareth,*
> *as Beastly Cold as Bard may be,*
> *who Next-to-Nothing weareth.*
>
> *Genius, ah, hath deck'd his Song,*
> *but oh, th' Ingratitude!*
> *Whilst other Blokes be warm as Toast,*
> *the Poet's damn near Nude.*

You catch my drift?                     *[handwritten: makes fun of poetry]*

PISTHETAIROS

>            Yes, I catch your drift.
You want some underwear.

*To the Acolyte.*

>                     All right, off with it, lad.
We can't allow our delicate poets to freeze to death.
And now clear out, will you?

POET

>                     I go, I go,
but first my final valediction to this little village—

*Singing.*

> *O Muse on golden throne,*
> *Muse with chattering teeth*

> *sing this capitol of cold,*
> *this frigorifical city!*

*I have been where the glebe is frozen with frore.*
*I have traipsed where the furrows are sown with snow.*
> > > > > *Alalai!*

> > > > > > > *Alalai!*

> > > > > > > > > *G'bye.*

*Exit Poet.*

PISTHETAIROS

Well, how do you like that? Griping about the cold
after making off with an entire new winter outfit!
And how in the name of heaven did that poetic plague
discover us so fast?

*To the naked and shivering Acolyte.*

> > > —You there, to work again.
Take up your laver and circle the altar, boy,
and we'll resume our inaugural sacrifice once again.
Quiet now, everyone.

*As Pisthetairos approaches the altar with the sacrificial knife,*
*an itinerant Prophet with a great open tome of oracles makes*
*his appearance.*

PROPHET

> > > HALT! Forbear, I say!
Let no one touch the victim.

PISTHETAIROS

> > > Who the hell are you,
may I ask?

PROPHET

> I am a Prophet, sir, in person.

PISTHETAIROS

> > > Then beat it.

PROPHET

Ah, the naughty wee scamp.

But we mustn't scoff.
Friend, I have brought you an oracle of the prophet Bakis,
transparently alluding to the city of Cloudcuckooland.

PISTHETAIROS

Why did you wait till after I founded my city
before disgorging this revelation of yours?

PROPHET

Alas,
I could not come. The Inner Voice said No.

PISTHETAIROS

I suppose we'll have to hear you expound your oracle.

PROPHET

Listen—
LO, IN THAT DAY WHEN THE WOLF AND THE
   CROW DO FOREGATHER AND COMPANION,
AND DOMICILE IN THE AIR, AT THAT POINT
   WHERE KORINTH KISSETH SIKYON*—

PISTHETAIROS

Look here, what has Korinth got to do with me?

PROPHET

Why,
it's ambiguous, of course. Korinth signifies "air."

*Resuming.*
PRESENT, I SAY, A WHITE SHEEP TO PANDORA,
BUT TO THE SEER WHO BRINGS MY BEHEST:
*IN PRIMIS*, A WARM WINTER COAT
   PLUS A PAIR OF SANDALS (THE BEST)—

PISTHETAIROS

The *best* sandals, eh?

PROPHET

>Yup. Look in the book.

*Resuming.*

>ITEM, A GOBLET OF WINE,
>ITEM, A GIBLET OF GOAT—

PISTHETAIROS

Giblet? It says giblet?

PROPHET

>Yup. Look in the book.

*Resuming.*

>IF, O BLESSÈD YOUTH, THOU DOST AS I ENJOIN,
>REGAL EAGLE WINGS THIS VERY DAY ARE
>    THINE.*
>NOT SO MUCH AS PIGEON FLUFF, IF THOU
>    DECLINE.

PISTHETAIROS

It really says that?

PROPHET

>Yup. Look in the book.

PISTHETAIROS

*Drawing out a huge tome from under his cloak.*

You know, your oracles somehow don't mesh with mine,
and I got these from Apollo's mouth.

>                                Listen—
>LO, IF IT CHANCE THAT SOME FAKER INTRUDE,
>TROUBLING THY WORSHIP AND SCROUNGING
>    FOR FOOD,
>        LET HIS RIBS BE BASHED
>        AND HIS TESTICLES MASHED—

PROPHET

I suspect you're bluffing.

PISTHETAIROS

Nope. Look in the book.

*Resuming.*

SMITE ON, I SAY, IF ANY PROPHET SHOULD
   COME,
YEA, THOUGH HE SOARETH LIKE THE SWALLOW.
FOR THE GREATER THE FAKER,* THE HARDER
   HIS BUM
SHOULD BE BATTERED.

                              GOOD LUCK.
                                    Signed,
                                       APOLLO.

PROPHET

Honest? It says that?

PISTHETAIROS

                  Yup. Look in the book.

*Suddenly throwing his tome at him and beating him.*

Take that!
         And that!
                  And that!

PROPHET

                  Ouch. Help!

PISTHETAIROS

Scat. Go hawk your prophecies somewhere else.

*Exit Prophet. From the other side enters the geometrician and surveyor Meton,* his arms loaded with surveying instruments.*

METON

The occasion that hath hied me hither—

PISTHETAIROS

                              Not another!

State your business, stranger. What's your racket?
What tragic error brings you here?

METON

                                    My purpose here
is a geodetic survey of the atmosphere of Cloudcuckooland
and the immediate allocation of all this aerial area
into cubic acres.

PISTHETAIROS

                  Who are *you?*

METON

                        Who am *I?*
Why, Meton, of course. Who else could *I* be?
Geometer to Hellas by special appointment.
Also Kolonos.

PISTHETAIROS

              And those tools?

METON                           *makes fun of science*
                              Celestial rules,
of course.
              Now attend, sir.
                              Taken *in extenso,*
our welkin resembles a cosmical charcoal-oven*
or potbellied stove worked by the convection principle,
though vaster. Now then, with the flue as my base,
and twirling the calipers thus, I obtain the azimuth,
whence, by calibrating the arc or radial sine—
you follow me, friend?

PISTHETAIROS

                        No, I don't follow you.

METON

No matter. Now then, by training the theodolite here
on the vectored zenith tangent to the Apex A,

I deftly square the circle, whose conflux, or C,
I designate as the center or axial hub of Cloudcuckooland,
whence, like global spokes or astral radii,
broad boulevards diverge centrifugally, forming,
as it were—

PISTHETAIROS

   Why, this man's a regular Thales!

*Whispering confidentially.*

Pssst. Meton.

METON

   Sir?

PISTHETAIROS

    I've taken quite a shine to you.
Take my advice, friend, and decamp while there's still time.

METON

You anticipate danger, you mean?

PISTHETAIROS

      The kind of danger
one meets in Sparta. You know, nasty little riots,
a few foreigners beaten up or murdered, knifings,
fighting in the streets and so on.

METON

     Dear me, you mean
there might actually be revolution?

PISTHETAIROS

     I certainly hope not.

METON

Then what *is* the trouble?

PISTHETAIROS

The new law. You see,
attempted fraud is now punishable by thrashing.

METON *be did fraud - real life*

Er, perhaps I'd best be going.

PISTHETAIROS

I'm half afraid
you're just a bit too late.
Yes!
Look out!
Here comes your thrashing!

*He batters Meton with a surveying rod.*

METON

HALP! MURDER!

PISTHETAIROS

I warned you. Go survey some other place, will you?

*Exit Meton. From the other side enters an Inspector,* dressed
in a magnificent military uniform and swaggering imperiously.*

INSPECTOR *government*

Fetch me the Mayor, yokel.

PISTHETAIROS

Who's this pcpinjay?

INSPECTOR

Inspector-general of Cloudcuckooland County, sir,
invested, I might add, with plenary powers—

PISTHETAIROS

Invested?

On whose authority?

INSPECTOR

Why, the powers vested in me
by virtue of this piddling piece of paper here
signed by one Teleas of Athens.

PISTHETAIROS

Look. Let me propose
a little deal, friend. I'll pay you off right now,
provided you leave the city.

INSPECTOR

A capital suggestion.
As it so happens, my presence is urgently required
at home. They're having one of their Great Debates.
The Persian crisis, you know.*

PISTHETAIROS

Really? Splendid.
I'll pay you off right now.

*Violently beating the Inspector.*

Take that!
And that!

INSPECTOR

What does this outrage mean?

PISTHETAIROS

The payoff. Round One
of the Great Debate.

INSPECTOR

But this is mutiny! Insubordination!

*To the Chorus.*

Gentlemen, I call on you Birds to bear me witness
that this man wilfully assaulted an Inspector.

PISTHETAIROS

Shoo, fellow,
and take your ballot boxes with you* when you go.

*Exit Inspector.*

What confounded gall! Sending us one of their Inspectors
before we've even finished the Inaugural Service.

*Enter an itinerant Legislator* reading from a huge volume of
laws.*

LEGISLATOR    more gov.

BE IT HEREBY PROVIDED THAT IF ANY CLOUD-
CUCKOOLANDER SHALL WILFULLY INJURE OR
WRONG ANY CITIZEN OF ATHENS—

PISTHETAIROS

Gods, what now? Not *another* bore with a book?

LEGISLATOR    bureaucrate

A seller of laws and statutes, sir, at your service.
Fresh shipment of by-laws on special sale
for only—

PISTHETAIROS

Perhaps you'd better demonstrate your wares.

LEGISLATOR

*Reading.*

BE IT HEREBY PROVIDED BY LAW THAT FROM
   THE DATE SPECIFIED BELOW
THE WEIGHTS AND MEASURES OF THE CLOUD-
   CUCKOOLANDERS ARE TO BE ADJUSTED
TO THOSE IN EFFECT AMONG THE OLOPHYX-
   IANS—

PISTHETAIROS

*Pummelling him*

By god, I'll Olo-phyx you!

LEGISLATOR

Hey, mister, stop!

PISTHETAIROS

Get lost, you and your laws, or I'll carve mine
on the skin of your tail.

*Exit Legislator. Enter Inspector.*

INSPECTOR

I summon the defendant Pisthetairos
to stand trial in court on charges of assault and battery
not later than April.

PISTHETAIROS

Good gods, are *you* back too?

*He thrashes Inspector who runs off. Re-enter Legislator.*

LEGISLATOR

IF ANY MAN, EITHER BY WORD OR ACTION, DO
   IMPEDE OR RESIST
A MAGISTRATE IN THE PROSECUTION OF HIS
   OFFICIAL DUTIES, OR REFUSE
TO WELCOME HIM WITH THE COURTESY PRE-
   SCRIBED BY LAW—

PISTHETAIROS

Great thundery Zeus, are *you* back here too?

*He drives the Legislator away. Re-enter Inspector.*

INSPECTOR

I'll have you sacked. What's more, I'm suing you
for a fat two thousand.

PISTHETAIROS

By Zeus, I'll fix you
and your blasted ballot boxes once and for all!

*Exit Inspector under a barrage of blows. Re-enter Legislator.*

LEGISLATOR

Remember that evening when you crapped in court?

PISTHETAIROS

                                                        Dammit.

Someone arrest that pest!

*Exit Legislator.*

                              And this time stay away!
But enough's enough.
                          We'll take our goat inside
and finish this sacrifice in peace and privacy.

*Exit Pisthetairos into house, followed by Acolyte with basket
and slaves with the sacrifice.*

CHORUS*

*Wheeling sharply and facing the audience.*

> Praise Ye the Birds, O Mankind!
>     Our sway is over all.
> The eyes of the Birds observe you:
>     we see if any fall.
>
> We watch and guard all growing green,
>     protecting underwing
> this lavish lovely life of earth,
>     its birth and harvesting.
>
> We smite the mite, we slay the pest,
>     all ravagers that seize
> the good that burgeons in your buds
>     or ripens on your trees.
>
> Whatever makes contagion come,
>     whatever blights or seeks
> to raven in this green shall die,
>     devoured by our beaks.

KORYPHAIOS

You know, gentlemen, that proclamation that's posted
  everywhere in town—

WANTED, DEAD OR ALIVE! DIAGORAS OF MELOS.
ONE TALENT'S REWARD FOR ANY MAN WHO
  KILLS THE TYRANT!
Well, we Birds have published our own public procla-
  mation:—
"HEAR YE!

*WANTED DEAD OR ALIVE!*
PHILOKRATES
  THE BIRDSELLER!
DEAD, 1 TALENT'S REWARD. 4 TALENTS IF
TAKEN ALIVE,
       BUT PROCEED WITH CAUTION. THIS MAN
IS DANGEROUS.
WANTED FOR MURDER AND CRUELTY TO BIRDS
  ON THE FOLLOWING COUNTS:—
  For the Spitting of Finches, seven to a skewer;
  *item*, for Disfiguring Thrushes by means of inflation;
  *item*, for Insertion of Feathers in Blackbirds' nostrils;
  *item*, for Unlawful Detention of Pigeons in Cages;
  *item*, for Felonious Snaring of Innocent Pigeons;
  *item*, for Flagrant Misuse of Traps and Decoy-devices."
So much for Philokrates.
                    But as for you, dear spectators,
we give you solemn warning.
                    If any boy in this audience
has as his hobby the keeping of Birds in captivity or cages,
we urgently suggest that you let your pets go free. Disobey,
and we'll catch *you* and lock you up in a wicker cage
or stake you out to a snare as a little decoy boy!

CHORUS       *Glorification of Birds*

    How blessèd is our breed of Bird,
        dressed in fluff and feather,
    that, when hard winter holds the world,
        wears no clothes whatever.

    And blazoned summer hurts no Bird,
        for when the sun leaps high,
    and, priestly in that hellish light,
        the chaunting crickets cry,

> the Birds keep cool among the leaves
> or fan themselves with flight;
> while winter days we're snug in caves
> and nest with nymphs at night.

> But Spring is joy, when myrtle blooms
> and Graces dance in trio,
> and quiring Birds cantatas sing
> *vivace e con brio.*

KORYPHAIOS

Finally, gentlemen, a few brief words about the First Prize
and the striking advantages of casting your vote for *THE
BIRDS* of Aristophanes—
advantages compared to which that noble prince,
poor Paris of Troy, was very shabbily bribed
indeed.
          First on our list of gifts comes a little item
that every judge's greedy heart must be panting to possess.
I refer, of course, to those lovely little owls of Laurium,
sometimes called the coin of the realm.
                              Yes, gentlemen,
these lovely owls, we promise, will flock to you by the
thousand, settle down in your wallets for good and hatch
you a brood of nice little nest eggs.
                    Secondly, gentlemen, we promise
to redesign your houses.
                    See, the sordid tenements vanish,
while in their place rise splendid shrines whose dizzy
heights, like Eagle-eyries,* hang in heaven.
                         Are you perhaps
a politician faced with the vexing problem of insufficient
plunder? Friend, your problems are over. Accept as our gift
to you a pair of Buzzard claws designed with special hooks
for more efficient grafting.
                    As for heavy eaters,
those suffering from biliousness, heartburn, acid indigestion
or other stomach ailments and upsets, we proudly present
them

with special lifetime Bird-crops, guaranteed to be virtually
indestructible.

    *If,* however, gentlemen, you withhold your vote,
you'd better do as the statues do and wear a metal lid
against our falling guano.

        I repeat.

            Vote against *THE BIRDS,*
and every Bird in town will cover you with—vituperation!

*The Chorus turns and faces the stage. Enter Pisthetairos.*

PISTHETAIROS

Birds, the omens are favorable. Our sacrifice has been
auspicious. But I wonder where in the world our messenger
is with news about our wall.

*A sound of furious panting offstage.*

        Aha. There he is now.
I'd recognize that awful huffing and puffing anywhere.
Those are the true Olympic pants and puffs I hear.

*Enter Messenger, panting.*

MESSENGER

Where anh where hoo where uh where can he be?
Where is Pisthetairos hanh?

PISTHETAIROS

        Here hunh here.

MESSENGER

Whew, the wall's all up! The wall's done!

PISTHETAIROS

           Splendid!

MESSENGER

What a wonderful, whopping, well-built wall! Whew!
Why, that wall's so wide that if you hitched up
four Trojan Horses to two huge chariots

with those braggarts Proxenides in one and Theogenes in the
  other,
they could pass head-on. *That's* the width of your wall!

**PISTHETAIROS**

Wow, what a width!

**MESSENGER**

                And what a height! Measured it myself.
Six hundred feet high!

**PISTHETAIROS**

                Poseidon, what a height!
Who in the world could have built a wall like that?

**MESSENGER**

The Birds.
            Nobody but Birds.
                        Not one Egyptian.
No bricklayers. No carpenters. Or masons.
Only the Birds. I couldn't credit my eyes.
What a sight it was:
                Thirty thousand Cranes
whose crops were all loaded with boulders and stones,*
while the Rails with their beaks blocked out the rocks
and thousands of Storks came bringing up bricks
and Plovers and Terns and seabirds by billions
transported the water right up to the sky!

**PISTHETAIROS**

                                Heavens!
But which Birds hauled the mortar up?

**MESSENGER**

                            Herons,
in hods.

**PISTHETAIROS**

    But how was the mortar heaped in the hods?

MESSENGER

Gods, now *that* was a triumph of engineering skill!
Geese burrowed their feet like shovels beneath
and heaved it over their heads to the hods.

PISTHETAIROS

They did?

Ah Feet! Ah, Feet! O incredible feat!*
What can compete with a pair of feet?

MESSENGER

And, sir,
you should have seen the Ducks with their aprons on
go hauling the bricks! And how the Swallows came
swooping, dangling their trowels behind them like boys,
and darting and dipping with mouthfuls of mortar!

PISTHETAIROS

Why,
if this is true, then human labor is obsolete.
But what happened next? Who finished off the job?
Who did the woodwork on the wall?

MESSENGER

Mastercraftsmen birds.
It was Pelicans, like carpenters, with handy hatchet-beaks
who hewed the gates, and what with the racket and hubbub
of all that hacking and chopping and hewing and banging,
sir, you'd have sworn it was a shipyard down at the docks.
Or so it sounded to me.
                              But the gates are done,
the bolts shot home, watchbirds make their rounds
with clanging bells, the guards patrol their beats
and every tower along the circuit of the wall
blazes with its watchfire. And in three words, sir,
all is well.
            But I must go and wash my face.
My job is done. The rest is up to you.

*Exit Messenger.*

KORYPHAIOS

Well,
wasn't it a wonder the way that wall of ours shot up?

PISTHETAIROS

A damn sight too wonderful. If you're asking me,
I think it's all a lie.
—But look what's coming:
another messenger, and a sentry judging by his looks.

*Enter Sentry, whirling on stage in the wild steps of a military dance.**

—What are you, fellow? A soldier or a ballerina?

SENTRY

ALAS! ALACKADAY!
OCHONE!
WOE IS ME!

PISTHETAIROS

Well, what's troubling *you?*

SENTRY

Sir, we are diddled
and undone.
Some god has given us the slip,
I wot not which. Carommed through the gates
out into territorial air. The Daws on guard
never spotted him.

PISTHETAIROS

Gad. A national scandal.
Which god?

SENTRY

We couldn't tell. But he was wearing wings,
that much we know.

PISTHETAIROS

Were Pursuitbirds sent up
to intercept him?

SENTRY

> Everything we had took off, sir.
> The Sparrowhawk Reserve, thirty thousand Falcons,
> every claw-carrying Harrier we could throw
> in the sky:—Kestrels, Buzzards, Owls, Eagles,
> Vultures, you name it.
> > Why, the whole atmosphere
> is throbbing and buzzing with the whirr of beating wings
> as they comb the clouds for that sneaky little god.
> If you're asking me, he's not so far away either.
> He's hereabouts. I'm sure.

*Exit Sentry.*

PISTHETAIROS

> > Where's my bow?
> Bring me my sling!
> > Archerbirds, fall in!
> Now shoot to kill.
> > Dammit, where's my sling?

CHORUS

> > Now words are weak
> > and ACTIONS speak
> > ineffably of War.
>
> > Let every Bird
> > for battle gird:
> > the gods are at our door:
>
> > Rise up, defend
> > your native land!
> > Go mobilize the Air!
>
> > Immortal spies
> > now prowl our skies.
> > And saboteurs. Take care.

KORYPHAIOS

> Quiet.
> I hear the whirr of beating wings.
> Listen. Some god comes whizzing through our air.

*With a loud whoosh and a burst of baroque movement and color, Iris descends in the machine. She is a young girl with golden wings and billowing rainbow-colored robes. From her dress and hair, in gracious and extravagant loops of color, pennants and ribbons and streamers trail out behind.*

PISTHETAIROS

Ship ahoy!
          Belay!
                    Where are you cruising?
Down anchors!
                    And stop luffing those wings.
Now who are you? Home Port? Purpose of voyage?

IRIS

I am Iris the fleet.

PISTHETAIROS

                    Clippership or sloop?

IRIS

What does this mean?

PISTHETAIROS

                    Some Buzzard flap up
and arrest that bitch.

IRIS

                    You dare arrest *me?*
What sort of joke is this?

PISTHETAIROS

                    You'll see, sister.

IRIS

But I must be dreaming. This can't be real.

PISTHETAIROS

What gate did you enter by? Answer, you slut.

**IRIS**

Gates? What would a goddess know about gates?

**PISTHETAIROS**

A glib little piece. Just listen to those lies.
—Well, did you report to the Daw on duty at the gate?
Mum, eh?
      Where's your Storkpass?

**IRIS**

                *I* must be mad.

**PISTHETAIROS**

What? You never even applied?

**IRIS**

              *You* must be mad.

**PISTHETAIROS**

Was your form filled out by Colonel Cock
and properly punched?

**IRIS**

           Just let him try!
Why, the very idea!

**PISTHETAIROS**

          So that's your game, is it?
To sneak in here, infiltrate our territorial air,
spy on our city—

**IRIS**

      But where can a poor god go?

**PISTHETAIROS**

How should I know? But not here, by god!
You're trespassing. What's more, it would serve you right
if I ordered you put to death this very instant.
If ever a god deserved to die, that god is you.

IRIS

But I *can't* die.

PISTHETAIROS

Well, you damn well should.
A pretty pickle it would be if the whole world
obeyed the Birds while you gods got uppity
and defied your betters.
Now then, you aerial yacht,
state your business here.

IRIS

*My* business? Why,
I am bearing the following message from my father Zeus
to mankind:
"LET HOLOCAUSTS MAKE GLAD THY
GODS AND MUTTON BARBECUES ON BEEFY
ALTARS TOAST, YEA, TILL EVERY STREET DOTH
REEK WITH ROAST AMBROSIALLY."

PISTHETAIROS

Hmm. I think he wants a sacrifice.
But to which gods?

IRIS

To *which* gods? To *us,* of course.
Who else could he mean?

PISTHETAIROS

But that's quite absurd.
*You,* gods? I mean, really!

IRIS

Name me any other gods.

PISTHETAIROS

Why, the Birds, madam. Birds are now the gods.
Men worship Birds, not gods. Good gods, no!

IRIS

*In the high tragic manner.**

Then beware, O Mole, lest thou court the choler
of the gallèd gods, and Justice with the angry pick
of peevèd Zeus prise up thy pedestals
and topple all thy people, leaving not a smitch;
yea, and forkèd levin sear thee to a crisp,
lambasted low amongst thy mortal porticoes
by lightnings blunderbuss'd, yea—

PISTHETAIROS

                         Listen, lady,
stow that tragic guff. You're starting to slobber.
And kindly stop twitching.
                         What do you think I am?
Some poor Lydian or Phrygian slave* you can browbeat
with that bogey-talk?
                         Go back and tell your Zeus
if he messes around with me, I'll fry him to a cinder!
What doth the poet say?*
    *Aye, with eagles belching levin,
    I shall scorch the halls of heav'n,
    till Zeus doth frizzle in his juice
    and Amphion, e'en Amphion—*
                         —But what am I saying?
How does Amphion fit in here?
                         Well, no matter.
But you tell your Zeus that if he crosses me, by god,
I'll send six hundred Porphyrions up against him,
and every Bird-Jack of the lot tricked out as a panther.
I'd like to see his face. I remember the time
when one poor piddling little Porphyrion
was one too many for Zeus.
                         But as for *you*,
Miss Messenger Iris, sail my way once more
and I'll lay my course right up your lovely legs,
and board you at the top.
                         Mark my words:
you'll be one flabbergasted little goddess
when you feel the triple ram on this old hulk.

**IRIS**

What a disgusting way to talk.

**PISTHETAIROS**

Skedaddle, slut.

**IRIS**

Just you wait till my Father hears about this.

**PISTHETAIROS**

Heaven defend me from this flying flirt. Beat it!
Go singe some youngster with your lechery, will you?

*Exit Iris in the machine.*

**CHORUS**

The gods' attack
has been rolled back,
    rebuffed by our Blockade.

Let god and man
now heed our ban:
    NO TRANSETHEREAL TRADE!

No more, no more
do victuals soar;
    no savory ascends;

and chops and stew
are now taboo:
    the party's over, friends!

**PISTHETAIROS**

You know, its rather odd about that other messenger
we despatched to earth. He should be back by now.

*Enter Herald in great haste. He throws himself to the ground
at Pisthetairos' feet and salaams profoundly.*

**HERALD**

O Pisthetairos! O Paragon! O Pink!
Thou Apogee of Genius! Sweet Flower of Finesse!

O Phoenix of Fame! Flimflam's Non-Pareil!
O of every noble attribute the Plus!
O Happy Happy Chap! O Blest! O Most!
O Best!—
        oh, balls.

PISTHETAIROS

        You were about to say, my friend,
when you so rudely interrupted yourself?

HERALD

*Rising and crowning Pisthetairos.*

Deign, my lord, to accept this crown of solid gold,
proffered in honor of your glorious wisdom and chicane
by an adoring world.

PISTHETAIROS

        I am deeply honored sir.
But why should man's election fall on me?

HERALD

O fabulous founder of great Cloudcuckooland,
how can you ask such a question? Have you not heard
that Pisthetairos has become the darling of the mortal
    world,
a name to conjure with? That all mankind
has gone Cloudcuckoolandophile,
madly, utterly?
        And yet, only yesterday,
before your dispensation in the skies became a fact,
the Spartan craze had swept the faddish world.
Why, men went mad with mimicry of Sokrates,*
affected long hair, indifferent food,
rustic walking sticks, total bathlessness,
and led, in short, what I can only call
a Spartan existence.
        But then suddenly, overnight,
the Birds became the vogue, the *dernier cri*
of human fashion.* And men immediately began
to feather their own nests; to cluck and brood;
play ducks and drakes; grub for chickenfeed;

hatch deals, and being rooked or gulled,
to have their little gooses cooked. But if they grouse,
they still are game.

In sum, the same old life,
but feathered over with the faddish thrills of being
chic.

But the latest word in Birds is names.
The gimpy peddler is tagged Old Partridge now;
Menippos is called Cuckoo; Opountios, Stool Pigeon;
Philokles is the Lark; Theogenes, the Pseudo-Goose;
Lykourgos, Lame Duck; Chairephon is Bats;
Syrakosios, of course, is called the Jaybird,
and as for Meidias, why, he's the Sitting Duck—
and judging from that ugly clobbered beak of his,
no man ever missed.

And that's not all.
Mankind has gone so utterly batty over Birds
that all the latest songs are filled with them—
Swallows, Pigeons, Ducks, Geese, you name it.
Any tune with feathers in it or a pinch or fluff
becomes a hit.

And that's how matters stand
below.

But one last point before I leave.
Vast swarms and coveys of men are on the move,
all migrating here to Cloudcuckooland in quest of wings
and the Feathered Way of Life. Somehow, sir,
you'll have to wing these mortal immigrants.

*Exit Herald.*

PISTHETAIROS

                                        Gad!
We'd best get busy.

*To a Slave.*

            —You there.
                        Run inside.
Stuff every hamper you can find with sets of wings
and tell Manes to bring them out. I'll stay here
to give my greeting to these wingless refugees in person.

*Exit Slave.*

CHORUS

> Upon thy head, Cloudcuckooland,
>     the crown of praise we set:
> O Beautiful for Swarming Skies—

PISTHETAIROS

> —Don't count your chickens yet.

CHORUS

> This feather'd isle, this pinion'd place,
>     where martyr-Birds have bled,
> where men aspire on wings of fluff—

*Enter Manes, slowly and empty-handed.*

PISTHETAIROS

> —Their legs are made of lead.

*Exit Manes.*

CHORUS

> What greater bliss can men require?
>     Here the lovely Graces go,
> and Wisdom strolls with sweet Desire,
>     and Peace comes tripping slow.

*Enter Manes carrying two wings.*

PISTHETAIROS

She's miles ahead of Manes.

> —Dammit, blockhead, move!

CHORUS

> To work, dull clod! Heave-ho the wings!

*Exit Manes.*
*To Pisthetairos.*

> Now show him you're the master.
> Flog him, thrash him—

*Enter Manes with two more wings.*

PISTHETAIROS

                              —What's the use?
    A mule could manage faster.

*Exit Manes.*

CHORUS

                    Now sort the wings in pinion-piles
                       by order of professions:
                    Seabirds' wings for nautical types,
                    Warblers' for musicians—

*Enter Manes with three wings.*

PISTHETAIROS

    —So help me, Kestrels, if I don't bash your head
       to a pulp, you lazy, stupid, bungling ass!

*Beats him. Manes scurries off, instantly reappearing with crates
and hampers of wings which he quickly dumps and sorts into
the appropriate piles. Suddenly from offstage is heard the tenor
voice of Delinquent, singing:*

             *If I had the wings of an Eagle,\**
    *o'er this barren blue brine I would fly . . .*

PISTHETAIROS

    That messenger of ours was telling the truth, by god.
    Here comes someone crooning Eagle-ballads.

*Enter Delinquent,\* a strapping boy in his teens.*

DELINQUENT

    Some kicks!
    There's nothin' on earth like flyin'! Whee!
                                        Chee,
    Cloudcuckooland's the roost for me! Hey, man,
    I'm bats about the Birds! I'm with it chum!
    I wanna be a Bird! I want your way of life!

PISTHETAIROS

    Which way? We Birds have bushels of ways.

**DELINQUENT**

If it's strictly for the Birds, then it's for me, man.
But best of all I like that splendid custom you've got
that permits a little Bird to choke his daddy dead.

**PISTHETAIROS**

True. We think it very manly of a young Bird
if he walks up and takes a poke at his old man.

**DELINQUENT**

                                        That's it, Dad.

Exactly why I'm here. I want to throttle
the old man and inherit his jack.

**PISTHETAIROS**

                    One moment.
We Birds observe another custom older still.
You'll find it preserved in the Scrolls of the Storks. I quote:
"ONCE THE AGÈD STORK HATH REARED HIS
    BROOD
AND HIS CHICKS HAVE MADE THEIR MAIDEN
    FLIGHT ALONE,
THEY MUST IN TURN SUPPORT THEIR FATHER IN
    HIS AGE."

**DELINQUENT**

A fat lot of good I've got from coming here, chum,
if I have to go back home and support the old man.

**PISTHETAIROS**

I tell you what. You seem a decent lad,
and I'll adopt you as our city's official Mascot-Bird.
But first some good advice I received as a toddler
at my mother's knee:
                    Don't drub your dad.
Take this wing instead.
                        With your other hand,
accept this spur. Here, your helmet is this crest.
Now march off, rookie. Drill, stand your guard,
live on your pay and let your father be.
You look aggressive: flutter off to Thrace.
There's fighting there.

DELINQUENT

By god, I think you're right.
What's more, I'm game.

PISTHETAIROS

You damn well better be.

*Exit Delinquent. From the other side enters the dithyrambic
poet Kinesias. His splay-footed galumphing entrance is in sharp
contrast to his aerial pretensions.*

KINESIAS

*On gossamer I go,
delicately wending,*/
up, up, up the airy stairs
of Poesy ascending—*

PISTHETAIROS

By god, we'll need a boatload of wings at least
to get this limping poet off the ground!

KINESIAS

*—forth through the Vast Unknown,
original, alone—*

PISTHETAIROS

Welcome, Kinesias, bard of balsa-wood!
What made you whirl your splay-foot hither, bard?

KINESIAS

*I yearn, I burn, thou know'st it well,
to be a lilting Philomel.*

PISTHETAIROS

A little less lilt, please. Could you stoop to prose?

KINESIAS

Wings, dull wight, wings!
Vouchsafe me wings
to percolate amidst the churning scud and rack

of yon conceited clouds from which I'll pluck and cull
tornado similes of blizzard speech.

**PISTHETAIROS**

You mean you plagiarize the clouds?

**KINESIAS**

                              Ah, my dear sir,
but our poet's craft depends completely on the clouds.*
Why, the most resplendent poem is but the insubstantial
shimmer refracted from that blue and bubbled murk of
froth, that featherfillip'd air.
                              Judge for yourself.

**PISTHETAIROS**

I won't.

**KINESIAS**

       Ah, but you shall, dear boy, you shall.
I'll do my Aerial Aria, and just for you.
                              Ready?

*Singing.*

              *Now wingèd wraiths*
              *of the hovering Plover*
              *over yon Ether rove—*

**PISTHETAIROS**

GALE WARNINGS POSTED! STAND BY, ALL SHIPS
   AT SEA!

**KINESIAS**

              *—over the billows pillow'd aloft,*
              *in the buffeting gust of the gathered gale—*

**PISTHETAIROS**

By god, I'll give you some buffets you won't like!

*He snatches a pair of large wings from a pile and beats Kinesias
who runs about, still spouting.*

KINESIAS

> *—now north, now south,*
> *and where they fare, fare I,*
> *cutting my wake*
> *on the harborless lake*
> *of the featherfillip'd sky.*

Get that, old boy? A catchy figure, what?

PISTHETAIROS

*Lashing him again.*

Get that? What? No taste for featherfillips, poet?

KINESIAS

What a beastly way to welcome a poetic genius
for whose services the entire civilized world competes!

PISTHETAIROS

Then stay with us. You can train an All-Bird
Chorus. Leotrophides will conduct his own compositions.
He likes the delicate stuff.

KINESIAS

> Durst despise me, sir?

Know then, I ne'er shall cease from Poesy
until with wings I waltz upon Cloudcuckooland.

> Farewell.

*Exit Kinesias. Enter an Informer in a tattered coat, singing.*

INFORMER

> *What suspicious Birds are these\**
> *that own no clothes and house in trees?*
> *O Cuckoo, Cuckoo, tell me true!*

PISTHETAIROS

We've passed the nuisance stage. This is crisis.
Here comes a warbler humming treason-trills.

INFORMER

Ho!

Again I cry:

*O Cuckoo, Cuckoo, tell me true!*

PISTHETAIROS

I think it must be an epigram on his tattered coat.
He's so cold he's calling the Cuckoo to bring the Spring.*
Poets are always talking out loud to Cuckoos in April.

INFORMER

You there. Where's the guy who's handing out the wings?

PISTHETAIROS

You're looking at him now. What do *you* want, friend?

INFORMER

Wings, fellow, wings! Got it?

PISTHETAIROS

I get it:
to hide the holes in your coat.*

INFORMER

*against spies*

Listen, Buster:
my business is the indictment of islands for subversive
activities.* You see in me a professional informer.

PISTHETAIROS

A splendid calling.

INFORMER

Also an *agent provocateur* of lawsuits and investigations.
That's why I want the wings. They'd come in handy
for whizzing around the islands delivering my indictments
and handing out subpoenas in person.

**PISTHETAIROS**

I see. And these wings would increase your efficiency?

**INFORMER**

Increase my efficiency? Impossible. But they'd help me dodge the pirates I meet en route. Then, coming home, I'd load the crops of the Cranes with writs and suits for ballast.

**PISTHETAIROS**

And *that's* your trade? A husky lad like yourself earning his livelihood by indicting foreigners?

**INFORMER**

But what am I supposed to do? I don't know how to dig.

**PISTHETAIROS**

Great Zeus Almighty, Aren't there enough honest means of earning a living without this dirty little dodge of hatching suits?

**INFORMER**

Listen, mister: it's wings I want, not words.

**PISTHETAIROS**

But my words *are* wings.

**INFORMER**

Your words are *wings?*

**PISTHETAIROS**

But of course. How else do you think mankind won its wings if not from words?

INFORMER

From words?

PISTHETAIROS

Wings from words.
You know the old men, how they loll around at the
  barbershop*
grousing and bitching about the younger generation?—
"Thanks to that damned Dieitrephes* and his damned
advice," growls one, "my boy has flown the family nest
to take a flier on the horses."
"Hell,"
pipes another, "you should see that kid of mine:
he's gone so damn batty over those tragic plays,
he flies into fits of ecstasy and gets goosebumps
all over."

INFORMER

And *that's* how words give wings?

PISTHETAIROS

Right.
Through dialectic the mind of man takes wing and soars;
he is morally and spiritually uplifted. And so I hoped
with words of good advice to wing you on your way
toward some honest trade.

INFORMER

It just won't work.

PISTHETAIROS

But why won't it?

INFORMER

I can't disgrace the family name.
We've been informers now for several generations,
you see.
So give me wings—Hawk's or Kestrel's
will suit me fine, but anything's all right by me
provided they're fast and light. I'll slip them on,

dart out to the islands with stacks of subpoenas and
summons, whizz back home to defend the case in court,
then zip right back to the islands again.

PISTHETAIROS

I get it.
When they arrive, they find their case is lost by default;
they've been condemned *in absentia*.

INFORMER

You've got it.

PISTHETAIROS

And while they're coming here, you're going there
to confiscate their property? Right?

INFORMER

You've got it.
I'll whirr around like a top.

PISTHETAIROS

Right. I've got it:
you're a top. And guess what I've got here for you:
a lovely little set of Korkyrean wings.

*He pulls out a whip.*

INFORMER

Hey, that's a whip!

PISTHETAIROS

Not a whip, it's wings
to make your little top go round.

*He lashes Informer with the whip.*

Got it?

INFORMER

Ouch! Owwooooo!

PISTHETAIROS

> Flap your wings, Birdie!
> That's it, old top, wobble on your way!
>
> By god,
> I'll make this legal whirligig go round!

*Exit Informer under the lash. Pisthetairos signals to his slaves to pick up the piles of wings.*

> —Hey,
> you there. Gather up the wings and bring them inside.

*Exeunt Pisthetairos and Attendants with the hampers of wings.*

CHORUS*

> Many the marvels I have seen,
>   the wonders on land and sea;
> but the strangest sight I ever saw
>   was the weird KLEONYMOS-tree.
>
> It grows in faraway places;
>   its lumber looks quite stout,
> but the wood is good for nothing,
>   for the heart is rotten out.
>
> In Spring it grows gigantic
>   with sycophantic green,
> and bitter buds of slander
>   on every bough are seen.
>
> But when, like war, cold winter comes,
>   this strange KLEONYMOS yields,
> instead of leaves like other trees,
>   a crop of coward's shields.
>
> And far away (but not so far),
>   we saw a second wonder,
> a place of awful, dismal dark—
>   when the sun goes under.
>
> And there by day dead heroes come
>   and talk with living men,
> and while it's light no ghost will hurt,
>   but when it's dark again,

> then thieves and ghosts take common shape,
>     and who knows which is which?
> So wise men dodge that dive at night—
>     but most of all the rich.
>
> For any man who ventures in
>     may meet ORESTES there,
> the ghost who paralyzes men,
>     the thief who strips them bare.

*Enter Prometheus,\* so muffled in blankets as to be completely unrecognizable. His every motion is furtive, but his furtiveness is hampered by an immense umbrella which he carries underneath his blankets. He speaks in a whisper.*

**PROMETHEUS**

Easy does it. I hope old Zeus can't see me.

*To a Bird.*

Psst. Where's Pisthetairos?

**PISTHETAIROS**

                    What in the world is *this?*
—Who are you, blanket?

**PROMETHEUS**

                    Shh. Are there any gods
on my trail?

**PISTHETAIROS**

            Gods? No, not a god in sight.
Who *are* you?

**PROMETHEUS**

            What's the time? Is it dark yet?

**PISTHETAIROS**

You want the time? It's still early afternoon.
Look, who the hell *are* you?

PROMETHEUS

                Is it milking-time, or later?

PISTHETAIROS

Look, you stinking bore—

PROMETHEUS

                What's the weather doing?
How's the visibility? Clear skies? Low ceiling?

PISTHETAIROS

*Raising his stick.*

                                By god,
if you won't talk—

PROMETHEUS

                Dark, eh? Good. I'm coming out.

*Uncovers.*

PISTHETAIROS

Hullo: it's Prometheus!

PROMETHEUS

                Shh. Don't make a sound.

PISTHETAIROS

What's the matter?

PROMETHEUS

                Shh. Don't even whisper my name.
If Zeus spots me here, he'll cook my goose but good.
Now then, if you want to learn the lay of the land
in heaven, kindly open up this umbrella here
and hold it over my head while I'm talking.
Then the gods won't see me.

*Pisthetairos takes the umbrella, opens it up, and holds it over Prometheus.*

PISTHETAIROS

Say, that's clever.
Prometheus all over.*
—All right. Pop underneath
and give us your news.

PROMETHEUS

Brace yourself.

PISTHETAIROS

Shoot.

PROMETHEUS

Zeus has had it.

PISTHETAIROS

Since when?

PROMETHEUS        *State of siege*

Since the moment
you founded the city of Cloudcuckooland. Since that day
not a single sacrifice, not even a whiff of smoke,
no savories, no roast, nothing at all
has floated up to heaven. In consequence, my friend,
Olympos is starving to death. And that's not the worst of it.
All the Stone Age gods* from the hill country
have gone wild with hunger, screaming and gibbering away
like a lot of savages. And what's more, they've threatened
war unless Zeus succeeds in getting your Bird-embargo lifted
and the tidbit shipments back on the move once more.

PISTHETAIROS

You mean to say there are *other* gods in Heaven?
Stone Age gods?

PROMETHEUS

Stone Age gods for Stone Age people.
Exekestides must have something to worship.

**PISTHETAIROS**

Heavens,
they *must* be savages. But what do you call them?

**PROMETHEUS**

We call them Triballoi.

**PISTHETAIROS**

Triballoi? From the same root
as our word "trouble," I suppose.

**PROMETHEUS**

Very probably, I think.
But give me your attention. At present these Triballoi gods
have joined with Zeus to send an official embassy
to sue for peace. Now here's the policy you must follow:
flatly reject any offers of peace they make you
until Zeus agrees to restore his sceptre to the Birds
and consents to give you Miss Universe* as your wife.

**PISTHETAIROS**

But who's Miss Universe?

**PROMETHEUS**

A sort of Beauty Queen,
the sign of Empire and the symbol of divine supremacy.
It's she who keeps the keys to Zeus' thunderbolts
and all his other treasures—Divine Wisdom, *Power*
Good Government, Common Sense, Naval Bases,
Slander, Libel, Political Graft, Sops to the Voters—

**PISTHETAIROS**

And *she* keeps the keys?

**PROMETHEUS**

Take it from me, friend.
Marry Miss Universe and the world is yours.
—You understand
why I had to tell you this? As Prometheus, after all,
my philanthropy is proverbial.

PISTHETAIROS

>               Yes, we worship you
> as the inventor of the barbecue.*

PROMETHEUS

>                       Besides, I loathe the gods.

PISTHETAIROS

> The loathing's mutual, I know.

PROMETHEUS

>                       Just call me Timon:
> I'm a misanthrope of gods.
>                       —But I must be running along.
> Give me my parasol. If Zeus spots me now,
> he'll think I'm an ordinary one-god procession. I'll pretend
> to be the girl behind the boy behind the basket.

PISTHETAIROS

> Here—take this stool and watch yourself march by.

*Exit Prometheus in solemn procession, draped in his blanket,
the umbrella in one hand, the stool in the other. Pisthetairos
and the Attendants retire.*

CHORUS*

>           There lies a marsh in Webfoot Land,
>               the Swamp of Dismal Dread,
>           and there we saw foul SOKRATES
>               come calling up the dead.
>
>           And there that cur PEISANDROS came
>               to see if he could see
>           the soul he'd lost while still alive
>               by dying cowardly.
>
>           He brought a special sacrifice,
>               a little camel lamb;
>           then, like Odysseus, slit its throat—
>               he slit its throat and ran!

And then a phantcm shape flew down,
a specter cold and wan,
and on the camel's blood he pounced—
the vampire CHAIREPHON!

*Enter the Peace Delegation from Olympos: first, Poseidon, a god of immense and avuncular dignity, carrying a trident; then Herakles with lion skin and club, a god with the character and build of a wrestler and an appetite to match; and finally Triballos, hopelessly tangled up in the unfamiliar robes of Olympian civilization.*

POSEIDON

Here we are. And there before us, ambassadors,
lies Cloudcuckooland.

*Triballos, by now hopelessly snarled up in his robes, trips and falls flat on his face.*

—Damn you! Back on your feet,
you hulking oaf. Look, you've got your robes
all twisted up.
No. Screw them around to the right.
This way. Where's your dignity, you heavenly hick?
O Democracy, I fear your days are numbered
if Heaven's diplomatic corps is recruited like this!
Dammit, stop twitching! Gods, I've never seen
a gawkier god than you!
—Look here, Herakles,
how should we proceed in your opinion?

HERAKLES

You hoid me,
Poseidon. If I had my way, I'd throttle the guy,
*any* guy, what dared blockade the gods.

POSEIDON

My dear nephew,
have you forgotten that the purpose of our mission here
is to treat for peace?

HERAKLES

I'd throttle him all the more.

*Enter Pisthetairos, followed by Attendants with cooking utensils. He pointedly ignores the presence of the Divine Delegation.*

**PISTHETAIROS**

*To Attendants.*

Hand me the cheese grater. Vinegar, please. All right,
now the cheese. Poke up that fire, somebody.

**POSEIDON**

Mortal, three immortal gods give you greeting.

*Dead Silence.*

Mortal, three immortal—

*justice of
divine and

**PISTHETAIROS**

Shush: I'm slicing pickles.

*lovely*

**HERAKLES**

Hey, what kind of meat is dat?

**PISTHETAIROS**

Those are jailbirds
sentenced to death on the charge of High Treason
against the Sovereign Birds.

**HERAKLES**

And dat luscious gravy
gets poured on foist?

**PISTHETAIROS**

*Looking up for the first time.*

Why hullo there: it's Herakles!
What do you want?

**POSEIDON**

Mortal, as the official spokesman
for the Divine Delegation, I venture to suggest that—

**PISTHETAIROS**

*Holding up an empty bottle.*

Drat it. We're out of oil.

HERAKLES

Out of oil?
Say, dat's a shame. Boids should be basted good.

POSEIDON

—As I was on the point of saying, official Olympos
regards the present hostilities as utterly pointless.
Further, I venture to observe that you Birds
have a great deal to gain from a kindlier Olympos.
I might mention, for instance, a supply of clean rainwater
for your Birdbaths and a perpetual run, say,
of halcyon days. On some such terms as these
we are formally empowered by Zeus to sign the articles
of peace.

PISTHETAIROS

Poseidon, you forget: it was not the Birds
who began this war. Moreover, peace is our desire
as much as yours. And if you gods stand prepared
to treat in good faith, I see no obstacle to peace.
None whatsoever. Our sole demand is this:
Zeus must restore his royal sceptre to the Birds.
If this one trifling concession seems agreeable to you,
I invite you all to dinner.

HERAKLES

Youse has said enough.
I vote Yes.

POSEIDON

You contemptible, idiotic glutton!
Would you dethrone your own Father?

PISTHETAIROS

I object, Poseidon.
Look at it in this light.
Can you gods be unaware
that you actually stand to increase, not diminish your power,
by yielding your present supremacy to the Birds? Why,
as things stand now, men go skulking around
under cover of the clouds, with impunity committing perjury

and in your name too. But conclude alliance with the Birds,
gentlemen, and your problems are over forever. How?
Suppose, for instance, some man swears a solemn oath
by Zeus and the Raven and then breaks his word. Suddenly
down swoops a Raven when he's least suspecting it
and pecks out his eyes!

POSEIDON

Holy Poseidon! You know,
I think you've got something there.

HERAKLES

Youse is so right.

POSEIDON

*To Triballos.*

What do you say?

TRIBALLOS

*Fapple gleep.*

HERAKLES

Dat's Stone Age for Yeah.*

PISTHETAIROS

And that's not all.
Suppose some fellow vows to make a sacrifice to the gods
and then later changes his mind or tries to procrastinate,
thinking, *The mills of the gods grind slow;
well, so do mine.*
We Birds, I can promise you,
will put a stop to sophistry like that.

POSEIDON

Stop it? But how?

PISTHETAIROS

Someday our man will be busily counting up his cash
or lolling around in the tub, singing away,
and a Kite will dive down like a bolt from the blue,
snatch up two of his sheep or a wad of cash
and whizz back up to the gods with the loot.

**HERAKLES**

Friend,
youse is right. Zeus should give dat sceptre
back to the Boids.

**POSEIDON**

What do *you* think, Triballos?

**HERAKLES**

*Threatening him with his club.*

Vote Yes, bub, or I'll drub youse.

**TRIBALLOS**

*Schporckl nu?*
*Momp gapa birdschmoz kluk.*

**HERAKLES**

See? He votes wid me.

**POSEIDON**

If you both see eye to eye, I'll have to go along.

**HERAKLES**

Dat does it. Hey, youse. The sceptre's yours.

**PISTHETAIROS**

Dear me, I nearly forgot one trifling condition.
We Birds willingly waive any claim we might have to Hera:
Zeus can have her. We don't object in the slightest.
But I must have Miss Universe as my wife. On that demand
I stand absolutely firm.

**POSEIDON**

Then you won't have peace.
Good afternoon.

*The Delegation prepares to leave, Herakles with great reluctance.*

PISTHETAIROS

It's all the same to me.
                              —Oh chef:
make the gravy thick.

HERAKLES

                    God alive, Poseidon, where in the
world is youse going? Are we going to war for the sake of a
dame?

POSEIDON

What alternative would you suggest?

HERAKLES

                              Peace, peace!

POSEIDON

You poor fool, don't you realize that you're being tricked?
What's more, you're only hurting yourself.
                              Listen here:
if Zeus should abdicate his throne in favor of the Birds
and then die, you'd be left a pauper. Whereas now
you're the legal heir of Zeus. Heir, in fact,
to everything he owns.

PISTHETAIROS

                    Watch your step, Herakles.
You're being hoodwinked.

*Taking Herakles by the arm and withdrawing a little.*

                    —Now, just step aside with me.
I have something to tell you.
                              Look, you poor chump,
your uncle's pulling a fast one. Not one cent
of Zeus' enormous estate will ever come to you
You see, my friend, you're a bastard.

HERAKLES

                              What's dat, fella?
*I'm a bastard?*

PISTHETAIROS

> Of course you're a bastard—by Zeus.
> Your mother, you see, was an ordinary mortal woman,
> not a goddess. In other words, she comes
> of foreign stock. Which makes you legally a bastard,*
> pure and simple.
>             Moreover, Pallas Athene
> is normally referred to as The Heiress.* That's her title.
> But how in the name of Zeus could Athene be an heiress
> if Zeus had any legitimate sons?

HERAKLES

>             Maybe.
> Youse could be right. But what if the Old Man
> swears I'm his son?

PISTHETAIROS

>          The law still says No.
> In any case, Poseidon here, who's been egging you on,
> would be the first person to challenge the will in court.
> As your father's brother, he's the next-of-kin, and hence
> the legal heir.
>             Let me read you the provisions of the law.

*He draws a lawbook from his robes.*

> In the words of Solon himself:
> SO LONG AS LEGITIMATE ISSUE SHALL SURVIVE
> THE DECEASED, NO BASTARD SHALL INHERIT.
> IN THE CASE THAT NO LEGITIMATE ISSUE SUR-
> VIVES, THE ESTATE SHALL PASS TO THE NEXT
> OF KIN.

HERAKLES

> Youse mean to say I won't inherit a damn thing
> from the Old Man?

PISTHETAIROS

*devine/rfd.*

> Not a smitch. By the way,
> has your Father ever had your birth legally recorded
> or had you registered in court as his official heir?

HERAKLES

No, never. I always thought there was something fishy.

PISTHETAIROS

Come, my boy, chin up. Don't pout at heaven
with that sullen glare. Join us. Come in with the Birds.
We'll set you on a throne and you can guzzle pigeon's milk
the rest of your endless days.

HERAKLES

                    You know, fella,
I been thinking about that dame you want so bad.
Well, I vote youse can have her.

PISTHETAIROS

                    Splendid.
What do you say, Poseidon?

POSEIDON

                    No. A resounding No.

PISTHETAIROS

Then it rests with Triballos.
                    —What's your verdict, my friend?

TRIBALLOS

*Gleep? Schnoozer skirt wotta twatch snock!
Birdniks pockle. Ugh.*

HERAKLES

                    He said she's for the Boids.
I hoid him.

POSEIDON

            And I distinctly heard him say the opposite:
A firm No—with a few choice obscenities added.

HERAKLES

The poor dumb sap never said a doity word.
All he said was: *Give 'er to the Boids.*

**POSEIDON**

I yield.
You two can come to terms together as you please.
Since you seem to be agreed on everything, I'll just abstain.

**HERAKLES**

*To Pisthetairos.*

Man, youse is getting everything youse wants.
Fly up to Heaven wid us, and get your missus
and anything else your little heart desires.

**PISTHETAIROS**

And we're in luck. This feast of poultry I've prepared
will grace our wedding supper.

**HERAKLES**

Youse guys push along.
I'll stay here and watch the barbecue.

**POSEIDON**

Not on your life.
You'd guzzle grill and all. You'd better come along
with us, my boy.

**HERAKLES**

Aw, Unc, but it woulda tasted so good.

**PISTHETAIROS**

*To Attendants.*

—You there, servants.
Bring my wedding clothes along.

*Exeunt Pisthetairos, the gods and Attendants.*

**CHORUS***

Beneath the clock in a courtroom,
down in the Land of Gab,
We saw a weird race of people,
earning their bread by blab.

Their name is the Claptraptummies.
   Their only tool is talk.
They sow and reap and shake the figs
   by dexterous yakkity-yak.

Their tongues and twaddle mark them off,
   barbarians every one;
but the worst of all are in the firm
   of GORGIAS & SON.*

But from this bellyblabbing tribe,
   one custom's come to stay:
in Athens, when men sacrifice,
   they cut the tongue away.

*Enter a Messenger.*

MESSENGER

O blessèd, blessèd, blessèd breed of Bird,
more happy than human tongue can tell:
welcome your lord and King as he ascends to heaven!
Attend him now!
                Praise him, whose glory glisters
more brightly than the rising stars at dusk
flare their loveliness upon the golden evening air,
purer than the blazoned sun!
                He comes, he comes,
and with him comes the splendid glory of a bride
whose beauty has no peer. In his hand he shakes
the wingèd thunderbolt at Zeus, the flash of lightning.
Unspeakably sweet, a fragrance ascends to heaven
and curls of incense trace their lovely spirals
on the drinking air.
                He comes!
                        Greet your King with song!
Raise the wedding song the lovely Muses sing!

*Re-enter Pisthetairos, gorgeously attired,\* his long golden train
carried by the three gods. Beside him, dressed in the magnificent golden robes of a bride, walks the veiled figure of Miss
Universe.*

KORYPHAIOS

Make way! Make way!
                Fall back for the dancers!

Welcome your King with beating wings!
Dance, dance!
Praise this happy Prince!
sing the loveliness of brides!
Weave with circling feet, weave and dance
in honor of the King, in honor of his bride!
Now let the Golden Age of Birds begin
by lovely marriage ushered in,
*Hymen Hymenaios O!*

CHORUS

To such a song as this,
the weaving Fates once led
the universal King,
Zeus, the lord of all,
to lovely Hera's bed.
*O Hymen! Hymenaois O!*

And blooming Love was there,
Love with shimmering wings,
Love the charioteer!
Love once held the reins,
Love drove the happy pair!
*O Hymen! Hymenaios O!*

PISTHETAIROS

I thank you for your songs and dance. Thank you, thank
you,
one and all.

KORYPHAIOS

Now praise the lightnings of your King!
Sing his thunders crashing on the world!
Sing the blazing bolts of Zeus, praise the man
who hurls them!
Sing the flare of lightning;
praise, praise the crashing of its awful fire!

CHORUS

O Lightning, flash of livid fire,
O javelin of Zeus,
everliving light!

*A great low roll of thunder is heard.*

> O thunders breaking on this lovely world,
> rumble majestic that runs before the rain!
> O Lightning and Thunders,
>                         bow low, bow down,
> bow before this man, bow to the lord of all!

*Another great crack of thunder.*

> He wields the thunder as his very own.
> Lightnings flare at the touch of his hand,
>                 winning, achieving
> the Bride of Heaven and the Crown of God!
>                 *O Hymen! Hymenaios O!*

**PISTHETAIROS**

> Now follow our bridal party, one and all.
> Soar on high, you happy breed of Birds,
> to the halls of Zeus, to the bed of love!

*He extends his hand to his bride and together they dance toward the waiting machine.*

>                 Reach me your hand, dear bride.
>                 Now take me by my wings,
>                 oh my lovely,
>                                 my sweet,
>                 and let me lift you up,
>                 and soar beside you
>                 through the buoyant air!

*Pisthetairos and his bride dance toward the waiting machine. With slowly beating wings they rise gradually heavenward. The gods and Attendants bow down in homage, the Chorus divides and flocks triumphantly toward the exits, chanting as they go.*

**CHORUS**

>                 *Alalalai!*
>                         *Io!*
>                                 *Paion!*
>                 O greatest of the gods!
>                 *Tenella Kallinikos O!*

# Notes

17. *A desolate wilderness:* The locale of the Hoopoe's nest belongs, of course, to the same fabulous geography as Cloudcuckooland itself. Since in mythology Tereus was the king of the Daulians, a Thracian people, the scene may be laid "somewhere in Thrace"—an extremely imprecise designation.

18. *even Exekestides couldn't do that:* Cf. Glossary, EXEKESTIDES. From the frequent allusions in the play to men who, technically ineligible, had somehow managed to get themselves enrolled as Athenian citizens, it is tempting to believe that proposals to revise the citizenship lists were in the air or had recently been carried out. The climax of these allusions comes in the final scene of the play, in which Pisthetairos attempts to prove that Herakles is technically a bastard (and hence cannot inherit Zeus' estate) because his mother was an ordinary mortal, i.e., of foreign stock.

19. *Old Tereus the bird who used to be a man:* Cf. Glossary, TEREUS.

    Despite the violent story which tells how Tereus became the Hoopoe, Prokne the Nightingale, and Philomela the Swallow, Aristophanes' Tereus and Prokne live happily together in marital bliss.

19. *this stinking, jabbering Magpie here:* In the Greek, the Magpie is actually called "son of Tharraleides." According to the Scholiast, Tharraleides' son was Asopodoros, a diminutive man commonly ridiculed as a runt. There may also be a pun on the word θαρραλέος, loquacious or impudent.

19. *dying to go tell it to the Birds:* Literally, the Greek says "dying to go to the crows," a common Athenian imprecation, and roughly equivalent to "go to perdition" or "go to hell" in English. Pisthetairos and Euelpides propose merely to follow the impre-

cation in its literal meaning—only to get lost en route.

19. Cf. Glossary, SAKAS and the note on *even Exekestides,* above.

20. *to pay their taxes:* A slight modernization of the Greek which says: "to pay fines."

20. *Because of legal locusts:* Aristophanes' favorite complaint against Athens, and one to which the entire *Wasps* is devoted. But although Aristophanes here develops Athens' love of litigation as the major source of dissatisfaction, elsewhere throughout the play the other grievances emerge: the restless and mischievous Athenian character (called πολυπραγμοσύνη); the plague of informers; the victimization of the Allies; the ambition for power, an ambition which knows no limits and whose only goal is World Mastery (βασιλεία).

20. *soft and lovely leisure:* Pisthetairos and Euelpides are looking, that is, for a place that offers them what Athens does not: release from the tortured, nervous, frenetic restlessness of Athenian life.

In Greek this quality of Athenian national restlessness was called πολυπραγμοσύνη, and its lexical meanings include "officiousness," "meddling," and "the activities of the busybody." Translated to social and political life, the word connotes those national characteristics which made the Athenians at once the wonder and the bane of the Greek world: national enterprise and energy vs. a spirit of unsatisfied restlessness; adventurous daring of action and intellect as against a spirit that seemed destructive of tradition and the life of rural peace; hunger for innovation and change undercut by the inability to temporize or be still. The word, in short, expresses precisely those qualities—daring, energy, ingenuity, strain, dynamic action, restlessness, ambition for acquisition and conquest, glory in change —that typify the Athens of the fifth century. It was these qualities that had made Athens great; they also made Athens imperial and thereby propagated themselves; they were responsible for the senseless protraction of the Peloponnesian War and they would, Aristophanes believed, eventually destroy

Athens as they had already destroyed the countryside of Attika and the virtue it fostered:
ἀπραγμοσύνη, the contented leisure of traditional
order and the rural conservatism of peaceful life.

The word is, of course, crucial to the play. For
if Aristophanes shows us in Pisthetairos here an
Athenian exhausted by years of national restlessness
and in search of ἀπραγμοσύνη among the Birds, it is
precisely his point that no Athenian can escape his
origin. And once arrived among the Birds, Pisthetairos promptly exhibits the national quality from
which he is trying to escape. He is daring, acquisi-
tive, ruthlessly energetic, inventive, and a thorough-
paced imperialist. And finally, in the apotheosis
that closes the play, he arrives at his logical desti-
nation—divinity. For πολυπραγμοσύνη, as Aristophanes ironically observed, is moved by nothing
less than man's divine discontent with his condition,
and the hunger of the Athenians to be supreme, and
therefore god.

20. *Try kicking the side of the cliff with your foot:* As
the Scholiast explains it, this line is an echo of a
children's jingle: "Kick the rock with your foot,
and the birds will fall down."

22. *I'm turdus turdus. An African migrant:* I have
taken a liberty here in an attempt to make English
of the Greek which literally says: "I'm a Scared-
stifflet. A Libyan species." *Turdus turdus* (the scientific name of the thrush) seemed to introduce the
right scientific note, as well as to accommodate the
obscenity which follows.

23. *I'm a Slavebird:* Cock-fighting cant. Greeks called
the loser in a cock-fight the "slave" of the winner.

24. *Right here in my hand:* If, as I suspect—contrary
to the belief of most scholars—the phallus was
worn in Aristophanic comedy, these words have
a point that is otherwise lacking. Pisthetairos, having let his bird escape, finds himself holding his own
phallus in terror. It is good fun based on good
observation.

25. *I'll bet the gods:* The Greek introduces the official
*Twelve* Gods here, probably for emphasis. I have
omitted them for clarity's sake.

25. *as the poet Sophokles disfigures me:* Sophokles had produced a tragedy called *Tereus* (lost) in which he may have described Tereus' metamorphosis into a Hoopoe. In the Aristophanic play, Tereus is obviously only slightly—and rather shabbily—metamorphosed, and he ascribes his shabbiness to his Sophoklean origins.

In appearance the European Hoopoe is a stunning and unusual bird, with brilliant black and white wing pattern and pink plumage and splendid black-tipped erectile crest.

26. *All Birds moult in winter:* With this statement the Hoopoe realistically accounts for his bedraggled plumage in March, when the play was performed.

26. *Then you must be jurymen:* The familiar taunt: everybody in Athens is on a jury.

26. *You can still find a few growing wild:* Aristophanes means that the only Athenians still untouched by the national disease of litigation were countrymen. The countryside breeds ἀπραγμοσύνη; the city, πολυπραγμοσύνη which finds expression in the suits brought by informers, etc.

27. *some country like a blanket, soft and snug:* ἀπραγμοσύνη again.

28. *court-officials with summons:* Euelpides is terrified by the thought of officials with summonses who may show up *anywhere* near the sea, even the Red Sea. The Greek mentions the "Salaminia," the galley used in Athens for official business, and the very vessel which had, a few months earlier, been despatched to Sicily with orders for the recall of Alkibiades to Athens to stand trial.

29. *If Opountios comes from Opous:* The pun here is untranslatable. Opountios was a one-eyed Athenian informer; Opous was a town in Lokris, and the word Oupountios designates an inhabitant of Opous as well as the Athenian informer.

29. *That's a honeymoon!:* Poppyseed was used in making wedding cakes, and myrtle berries were used for wedding wreaths.

30. *and people say:* In the manuscript it is Teleas—and not people—who sneers at the Birds. Teleas was evidently an extremely flighty and silly Athe-

nian official and Aristophanes' point is the obvious one: it takes a Bird to recognize a Bird.

31. *The heavens, you see, revolve upon a kind of pole:* This line and the three that follow it involve a series of untranslatable puns and some difficult scientific jargon. The Greek for "the vault of the heavens" is πόλος, which leads naturally to πολεῖται (revolves), which resembles πολῖται (citizens), which in turn yields πόλις (city). The argument is a fine specimen of sophistic doubletalk.

31. *wipe them all out by starvation:* The manuscript says literally, "wipe them out with a Melian famine." The year before the performance of *The Birds,* the small neutral island of Melos had been blockaded by an Athenian fleet and reduced by slow starvation. When finally captured, the entire male population was put to the sword and the women and children enslaved.

It is, of course, a deliberate part of Aristophanes' general ironic design that the tactics used by Pisthetairos against the gods are, in fact, the brutal military tactics of Athenian imperialism. However fantastic the play may seem, its purpose is the relentless satirical equation of Athens and Cloud-cuckooland.

36. *Like something out of Aischylos:* The line which follows is a quotation from the (lost) *Edonoi* of Aischylos.

37. *the son of the Hoopoe in Philokles' tragedy of* Tereus: The passage is a complicated one. But its basis seems to be an elaborate comparison between three generations of Hoopoes and three generations of the family of Kallias, and its point is surely (1) a charge of plagiarism against the tragedian Philokles and (2) the charge of profligacy against the younger Kallias.

There are three *Hoopoes:* (1) Hoopoe *grandpère* (the Hoopoe who married Prokne and the hero of Sophokles' *Tereus*); (2) Hoopoe *père* (the Hoopoe of Philokles' *Tereus,* a plagiarism of—and therefore descended from—Sophokles' play); and (3) Hoopoe *fils,* the dissolute and bedraggled Hoopoe of the Chorus. To these correspond: (1) Kallias

*grandpère,* a distinguished Athenian; (2) Hipponikos, son of Kallias (1), and also distinguished;
and (3) Kallias *fils,* the unworthy and profligate
scion of a distinguished line. (The family was
evidently addicted to alternating names with each
generation: Kallias, Hipponikos, Kallias, Hipponikos, etc.)

37. *our boy Kleonymos:* Kleonymos was a notorious
glutton and an equally notorious coward. Since
cowards have lost their crests (by throwing away
their helmets on the battlefield), the Crested
Guzzleguzzle should not be confused with Kleonymos.

38. *this crestwork on the Birds:* This joke depends
upon a pun on the word λόφος, which means:
(1) the crest of a bird, (2) the summit—or crest—
of a hill.

38. *Her lover. The Horny Pecker:* This is Arrowsmith,
not Aristophanes, and so too is the following line.
But the lines seemed to me utterly untranslatable
since they involved an impossible pun on the word
κειρύλος (which means both "kingfisher" and
"barber") and an obscure barber by the name of
Sporgilos. In the circumstances it seemed better
to betray the letter than the spirit.

39. *Bringing Owls to Athens:* The Athenian equivalent
of "bringing coals to Newcastle."

39. *I detect a note of menace:* The effect of the entire
following scene depends upon our understanding of
the *natural* hostility between Birds and Man (cf. 1.
369 ff.). In a country policed by the bird-loving
vigilantes of the Audubon Society, Aristophanes'
Birds might seem unreasonably hostile and suspicious of human motives. But anyone who has
ever seen a Mediterranean bird-market or been
offered pickled thrushes or *uccellini con polenta*
will understand. Those who do not are advised to
read closely the second Parabasis (1058 ff.) and to
ponder Pisthetairos' little poem at 523 ff. Seen in
the light of this total hostility, Pisthetairos' persuasion of the Birds is an extraordinary feat, designed,
I believe, in order to exhibit his characteristic Athenian resourcefulness and eloquence and cunning.

43. *Birds are skittish of platters:* In the Greek it is owls who are said to be skittish of platters. The reason for this skittishness is not known; it may be because owls are sacred to Athena and Athena was supposed to have invented the art of pottery. I preferred in the circumstances to emphasize the Birds' terror of becoming a meal.

44. *closely related to my wife:* Tereus' wife Prokne was Athenian and all Athenians regarded themselves as related by virtue of the very kinship-structure of the city.

46. *in Athens at public cost:* Soldiers who fell on the battlefield for Athens were buried at public expense in the Kerameikos outside the city.

46. *any reference to Birds:* Literally, the Greek says, "we will say that we died fighting the enemy at Orneai." "At Orneai" in the Greek is a pun on ὄρνις (bird), i.e., "at Birdland," and the town of Orneai which lay between Korinth and Sikyon and which, in 416, underwent a bloodless one-day siege.

48. *you know who I mean:* "The armor-making baboon" seems to have been a certain knife-maker called Panaitios who was married to an extremely promiscuous shrew. They managed to arrive at a marital *modus vivendi* only by making a formal compact of truce.

50. *Someone fetch water for my hands:* An orator put on a crown of myrtle before beginning his speech, but the wreath and the washing of hands are the customary preparations for a feast; hence Euelpides' question.

51. *Because you're a lazy Bird:* In the Greek κοὐ πολυπράγμων, uninquisitive, not on one's toes, sluggish, without curiosity. The Birds' fallen estate and decadence is directly traceable to their lack of πολυπραγμοσύνη, Pisthetairos' most outstanding trait. Cf. note on p. 136, *soft and lovely leisure*.

51. *And that's how Asbury got its name:* A complicated bit of foolery crowned by Euelpides' elaborate pun, which I have freely altered for the effect. Pisthetairos actually says that, according to "Aesop," the Lark buried her father in her own head. The word for "head" in Greek is κεφαλή, which is also the

name of an Athenian deme. Hense Euelpides' crack: the father of the Lark is buried at κεφαλή.

52. *and let the woodpeckers reign:* Since the oak tree was sacred to Zeus and the woodpeckers attacked the oaks, Zeus would be particularly unwilling to yield his sceptre to the Woodpecker.

53. *falling flat on your face whenever you saw a Kite:* The Kite was a harbinger of Spring, according to the Scholiast, and one which was evidently welcomed with almost religious joy.

53. *I swallowed my money:* It was common in antiquity for people to carry their coins in their mouth, probably as a precaution against theft.

54. *we still call the Egyptians cuckoo:* The cuckoo's call was in Egypt a call to reap, as Pisthetairos explains. To this Euelpides replies with a proverbial expression whose meaning is obscure—though almost certainly obscene. Since I could not translate what I could not understand, I have tried to make Euelpides' reply consistent with his zaniness elsewhere.

54. *on the rows where the politicians sit:* Literally, the Greek says that the birds on sceptres were keeping an eye on Lysikrates, to see whether he was bribed. Lysikrates was an Athenian general of a dishonest and corrupt character.

55. *Doctors still swear by the Duck:* A deliberate improvisation of my own to circumvent the complexity of the Greek. Literally, the line reads: "Lampon swears by the Goose when he's trying to cheat you." Lampon was a notorious soothsayer, but evidently superstitious enough that he tried to mitigate his perjury when fleecing a victim: instead of swearing an oath by Zeus (Zῆνα), he swore by the Goose (Xῆνα).

57. *A Babylon of the Birds!:* Cf. Glossary, BABYLON.

57. *each Bird must be paired with a god:* These pairs depend upon similarity in character or upon puns, and I have altered several of them accordingly. Thus in the manuscript Aphrodite is paired with the phalarope (which is suggested by *phallos*); Poseidon, god of the sea, is matched by a seabird;

the glutton Herakles by the cormorant; and Zeus, king of the gods, by the wren, king of the birds.

61. *"Five lives of men the cawing Crow outliveth":* A garbled echo of Hesiod, frag. 50.

61. *can strut on an olive limb:* The olive was sacred to Athena and hence should be acceptable even to aristocratic birds.

63. *Remember what old Aesop tells us:* According to the Scholiast, the fable should be ascribed to Archilochos rather than Aesop. But the gist of the fable seems to be as follows. The Fox and the Eagle swore lasting friendship and built their homes close together: the Eagle up in the tree, the Fox at the foot. During the Fox's absence one day, the Eagle swooped down, carried off the Fox's cubs, and proceeded to make a meal of them. The Fox, unable to climb the tree, could not take vengeance.

66. *The Chorus turns sharply and faces the audience:* The Parabasis, (or Digression), that part of an Aristophanic comedy in which the Chorus steps forth and addresses the audience directly, usually on behalf of the poet. In this play the Parabasis is linked with unusual coherence to the action, whereas in most comedies the Chorus employs the Parabasis to expound the topical social and political views of the comedian.

The opening anapestic section of the Parabasis is devoted to what might be called an Avine Cosmogony, a splendid and eloquent exposition of the origins of the world and the creation of the Birds and the gods. This defense of the antiquity of the Birds then passes into an overtly humorous bid for support, as though the Birds were campaigning for the votes which will make them gods. This is followed by a lovely lyric strophe ("O woodland Muse") which is succeeded by the *epirrhema* in a more topical and satirical vein; then the lyric antistrophe ("And so the swans") and the farcical *antepirrhema* ("You haven't really lived till you've tried a set of FEATHERS!").

The relevance of the opening cosmogony to the theme of the play has been questioned, but unreasonably I think. If Cloudcuckooland is an Athenian

Utopia, the meaning of Utopia is scored when
Pisthetairos achieves his apotheosis in the finale.
He has built Utopia by becoming god, and escaping
his human condition. It is to the reality and sadness of man's condition that the cosmogony of the
blessed Birds is addressed, and these lovely opening
lines ("O suffering mankind, lives of twilight, race
feeble and fleeting") are intended as a tragic coun-
terweight to the crazy comic dream of mankind
with which the play closes.

66. *tell Prodikos to go hang:* Prodikos was a sophist
whom Aristophanes seems to have respected. The
point here is that, wise as Prodikos may be, as a
teacher of truth he is not to be compared with
the Birds.

67. *laid her wind-egg there:* A wind-egg is an unfertil-
ized pullet's egg.

70. *the poet stole his honied song:* i.e., the tragic poet,
Phrynichos, famous for his lyric sweetness.

72. *Dieitrephes, our vulgar Ikaros of trade:* For
Dieitrephes, see Glossary. Aristophanes, like most
conservatives, is a convinced snob, and he almost
never forgives a man his business background, especially if the man has succeeded, as Dieitrephes
had, in making his way into the *élite* ranks of the
chivalry.

73. *the poor Birds in that Aischylos play:* A reference
to, followed by a quotation from, the lost *Myrmi-
dones* of Aischylos.

73. *insult my mattress by giving it a name like Sparta:*
A pun on Σπάρτη (Sparta and σπάρτη, a kind of
broom from which rope and bed-cording were
made). Euelpides detests Sparta so much that he
wouldn't attach σπάρτη to his bed.

74. *who will guard our Storkade?:* The wall which sur-
rounded the Akropolis of Athens was usually called
the Pelasgic Wall but sometimes the Pelargic Wall,
both related forms. Aristophanes here uses Pelargic
Wall, fancifully deriving it from πελαργός ("stork").
"Storkade" is B. B. Rogers' *trouvaille* and one
which I gratefully adopt here.

75. *Hop it, man!:* Pisthetairos' officiousness with Euelpides here is a stunning example of πολυπραγμοσύνη.

76. *Flutist, come in!* At these words the flutist Chairis, dressed as a Blackbird or a Crow, steps forward. Chairis' music seems to have grated intolerably on Aristophanes' ears; he is a *bête noire* in *The Acharnians* (425 B.C.) and still obnoxious by the time of *The Birds* eleven years later.

76. *propping his beak with a leather belt:* Evidently a mouth band or flutist's lip protector.

77. *the Bidding Prayer of the Birds:* This entire prayer is a parody of the customary invocation of the gods, in each case, by pun or burlesqued attributes or cult titles, linking a god with a bird. Because of the elaborateness of the puns and the obscurities of cult titles, literal translation is out of the question, and I have tried to make my own puns where I could not re-create the Greek—as I rarely could. Thus my Artemis is not a Finch but an American Phoebe, an appropriate name, I thought, for the sister of Phoibos; Kybele, Mother of Gods and Men, is not an Ostrich, as she is in the Greek, but a Dowitcher, a bird which suggested "dowager," and the Great Mother of Bustards. Those who are interested in discussion of the literal Greek should consult Roger's commentary on the passage.

78. *pray for the Chians too:* Cf. Glossary, CHIANS.

79. *as Homer hath it:* Everything about this poet is begged, borrowed, or stolen. Here he attributes lines to Homer which either are not Homeric or Homer so muddled as to be unrecognizable.

80. *O Father, Founder of Etna:* This whole passage is evidently a hideously garbled and atrociously adapted burlesque of Pindar's ode dedicated to the Syracusan tyrant Hiero on the founding of the town of Etna.

81. *Undressed amidst the nomad Skyths:* More Pindar, perhaps quoted almost verbatim, but doggerelized deliberately by me since no contemporary reader could be expected to recognize the Pindaric manner or its incongruous humor in this particular context.

83. *WHERE KORINTH KISSETH SIKYON:* That is, at Orneai. Cf. Note on p. 141, *any reference to Birds*. Itinerant prophets in Athens could live well by supplying ambiguous predictions of conquest

and victory to the ambitious Athenians. This particular prophet may very well be quoting from an actual oracle which predicted the sack of Orneai and thereby prompted the expedition; he then attempts to resell the same article, differently interpreted, to Cloudcuckooland.

84. *REGAL EAGLE WINGS THIS VERY DAY ARE THINE:* This is said to have been the favorite prediction of the Athenian Demos (cf. *Knights*, 1013). The Eagle, of course, symbolized supremacy and conquest.

85. *FOR THE GREATER THE FAKER:* The manuscript specifies by name two of these fakers. The first is Lampon, Athens' most renowned soothsayer; the second, Diopeithes, the accuser of the philosopher Anaxagoras.

85. *METON:* Cf. Glossary.

86. *our welkin resembles a cosmical charcoal-oven:* Meton's whole lecture is an elaborate spoof of technical "scientific" jargon of the age. But because Greek scientific jargon is almost chaste compared to our splendid modern proliferations, I have worked it up in order to create an effect analogous to that intended for Greek ears.

88. *enters an Inspector:* The Inspector, or Commissioner, was a regular Athenian official sent out from Athens to supervise subject states or to organize newly founded colonies. Their salaries seem to have been paid by the colonies they supervised, and some of them, like the Inspector here, had become rich men in the course of their careers.

89. *The Persian crisis, you know:* A free rendering. In the original the Inspector alludes loftily to his negotiations with the Persian satrap Pharnakes; he is needed at home for consultation about these weighty negotiations. Persia at this time, however, was more and more becoming a crucial factor in Greek political life.

90. *and take your ballot boxes with you:* Wherever Athenian inspectors are found, there will also be ballot boxes, the typical device of Athenian democracy, and arbitrarily instituted throughout the empire.

90. *Enter an itinerant Legislator:* During the war the Athenian Assembly had passed so many decrees, regulations, etc., that it became virtually impossible ·for the subject-cities and colonies to keep abreast of them. In the circumstances the practice of peddling the latest crop of statutes became a flourishing trade. ·

92. *CHORUS:* The second Parabasis: The Birds eulogize themselves and the blessings they bring, issue their own proclamation, and explain to the Judges the advantages of awarding *The Birds* the first prize.

94. *shrines whose dizzy heights, like Eagle-eyries:* In Greek the word ἀετός meant (1) an Eagle, and (2) the triangular pediment which crowned the pillars.

96. *Thirty thousand Cranes whose crops were all loaded with boulders and stones:* Cranes were believed to use stones to ballast themselves; the ballast was held in the crop.

97. *Ah Feet! Ah, Feet! O incredible Feat!* This is a common proverb with the word "feet" substituted for "hands."

98. *the wild steps of a military dance:* The *pyrrhichē* danced in full armor. Actually, the sentry is not dancing; the dancing is in his eyes, i.e., ablaze with martial ardor.

103. *In the high tragic manner:* Iris' tragic fulmination is probably a pastiche of all the tragedians, patched out with some Aristophanic inventions.

103. *Some poor Lydian or Phrygian slave:* A direct quotation from Euripides' *Alkestis*, 675.

103. *What doth the poet say?:* A quotation from the lost *Niobe* of Aischylos, incongruously incorporated into the passage without alteration. In order to clarify the deliberate incongruity (the mention of Amphion), I have intruded the line which follows the quotation.

105. *mimicry of Sokrates:* A gibe at the Spartan affectations of the Socratic circle and especially Sokrates' personal uncleanliness. To some extent this may be merely an exploitation of the common man's stereotype of the intellectual and philosopher. I remember

a Princeton landlady telling me that Einstein neve took a bath; this was her revenge on his genius. A for Sokrates, who knows?

105. *the dernier cri of human fashion:* The examples o the avine vogue which follow are all of my own in vention. The Greek cannot be literally translated int English because it is based upon an untranslatable pun (νομός, meaning both "law" and "pasture" o "feeding-place"), designed to parody, in avine terms, the Athenian love of litigation.

108. *If I had the wings of an Eagle:* A quotation, according to the Scholiast, from the lost *Oinomaos* of Sophokles.

108. *Delinquent:* The Greek is πατρολοίας, a word which it is usual to translate as "parricide," although it means merely "father-beater." Since our young man merely *wants* to murder his father, I have made him an adolescent punk and called him Delinquent.

110. *On gossamer I go, delicately wending:* According to the Scholiast, a parody of Anakreon.

111. *our poet's craft depends completely on the clouds:* For the Clouds as patron goddesses of dithyrambic poets, cf. *Clouds,* 335 ff. Poets whose compositions are a characteristic blend of obscurity, turbid emptiness and inflated language naturally depend upon the Murky Muse for inspiration.

112. *What suspicious Birds are these:* Adapted from a poem by Alkaios.

113. *he's calling the Cuckoo to bring the Spring:* In the Greek it is the Swallow who brings the Informer's Spring.

113. *to hide the holes in your coat:* Literally the manuscript has Pisthetairos say: "Are you planning to fly to Pellene?" Pellene was famous for its heavy woolen clothing, offered as prizes in the contests celebrated there.

113. *the indictment of islands for subversive activities:* By "islands" is meant the subject-states of the Athenian Empire, very largely comprised of the Aegean islands. Since the islanders were compelled to refer their more important lawsuits to the verdict of Athenian juries, they were therefore in a disadvan-

tageous position and easily victimized by professional informers.

115. *they loll around at the barbershop:* The barbershop was *par excellence* the nerve center of Athenian gossip, rumor, and political speculation.

115. *that damned Dieitrephes:* Cf. Glossary, DIEITREPHES. Dieitrephes was a notorious horse-racing enthusiast and hence in high favor with the wastrels among the Athenian *jeunesse dorée*.

117. *CHORUS:* With this strophe Aristophanes commences a series of brief Travelogues by the Birds: strange sights and marvels which their world-traveling has enabled them to visit. Actually, of course, all of the wonders are merely fabulized versions of familiar Athenian institutions and personages: the coward-sycophant Kleonymos, the thief Orestes, the psychagogue Sokrates and his accomplice Chairephon, the incredible tongue-worship of the wondrous men of Athens.

In this strophe Kleonymos is compared to a tree which grows enormous in the Spring and in winter sheds, not leaves, but shields. The Spring was the banner season for informers and sycophants, when men like Kleonymos (physically fat to begin with) were bloated with the profits of their trade. In winter the Kleonymos-tree sheds its shields, an allusion to Kleonymos' cowardice in battle (i.e., throwing down his shield and running away).

The second part of the strophe deals with the notorious footpad Orestes and concludes with a play on the name: (1) the Athenian thief, (2) his famous legendary predecessor, the son of Agamemnon. The point seems to be that those who venture out in Athens at night may meet Orestes the thief (who stripped his victims) or Orestes the heroic ghost (who paralyzed his victims—a power possessed by heroes, according to the Scholiast).

118. *Enter Prometheus:* Mankind's greatest champion and arch foe of Zeus makes his ridiculously furtive entrance on still another philanthropic mission: to warn Pisthetairos of Zeus' plans and secrets. Needless to say, he is extremely anxious to avoid observation by the gods.

120. *Say, that's clever. Prometheus all over:* Pisthetairos is impressed by the ingenuity of Prometheus' umbrella, and compliments him as deserving of his name (Prometheus meant "Foresight").

120. *All the Stone Age gods:* A free—but I thought plausible—rendering of the "barbarian gods" of the text. If Triballos is a representative of the barbarian gods, then the divinities meant are not merely uncivilized but Neolithic.

121. *Miss Universe:* The Greek gives βασιλεία, which means "sovereignty," "empire," "supreme power." Because she is an unfamiliar abstraction and not a genuine Olympian at all, I have felt free to turn her into a "sort of Beauty Queen" and to gloss her in the text as "the symbol of divine supremacy." In this play she symbolizes the logical conclusion of the Athenian (or the Birds') struggle for domination and universal supremacy. She is what Thoukydides called ἀρχή ("empire," "domination") and what I believe Euripides everywhere in his tragedies meant by the figure of Helen: the prize for which the (Peloponnesian) War was fought.

122. *the inventor of the barbecue:* Because Prometheus gave fire to man.

122. *CHORUS:* The second installment of the Birds' Travelogue. The subject is Sokrates as psychagogue or psychopomp, the guide of the soul, engaged in calling up spirits from the dead in a little sacrifice which resembles that of Odysseus in Book XI of the *Odyssey*. Sokrates' Stygian assistant is his cadaverous colleague of Athenian life, Chairephon.

   The scene takes place in the land of Shadowfeet (according to Ktesias, a curious web-footed tribe which lived in Libya; when they lay down for a nap, they held up their huge webfeet as awnings against the sun. To this the Scholiast adds that they had four legs, three of which were used for walking, and the fourth as a tentpole for their tentlike feet). Here, beside a Stygian swamp, haunted by terror, Sokrates summons the soul of Peisandros, an Athenian coward in search of his *psyche* (i.e., courage), by means of sacrifice; but so faint-hearted is Sokrates that he runs away in terror, leaving the bloody victim to the spectral vampire Chairephon.

126. *Dat's Stone Age for Yeah:* Cf. note on p. 150, *All the Stone Age gods.*

129. *Which makes you legally a bastard:* According to Athenian laws on citizenship, citizens must be born of Athenian fathers and mothers. Herakles, as the son of Zeus (a *bona fide* Olympian) and Alkmene (an ordinary woman, i.e., a foreigner) would be both illegitimate and ineligible for citizenship—according to Athenian law.

129. *Pallas Athene is normally referred to as The Heiress:* Because Athens was Athena's "portion," she was officially called The Heiress.

131. *CHORUS:* The concluding section of the Birds' Travelogue, a pointed satire on the Athenian worship of the Clacking Money-Making Tongue in thin anthropological disguise.

132. *of GORGIAS & SON:* To Gorgias the manuscript adds the name of Philippos, son or disciple of Gorgias the sophist. It was believed that the persuasive tongue of Gorgias served to stimulate the disastrous interest in Sicily among Athenians which culminated in the Sicilian Expedition.

132. *Re-enter Pisthetairos, gorgeously attired:* The culmination of the play in the aposthesosis of Pisthetairos and the marriage with Miss Universe. Man's comic dream is completed; by building Cloudcuckooland and winning Miss Universe, Man becomes supreme, escapes his mortal condition, and achieves divinity. It would be blasphemous if it were not so terribly ironic a wish-fulfillment of the god-intoxicated Athenian Dream.

# Glossary

AESCHYLUS, AISCHYLOS: The great Athenian tragedian (525-456 B.C.).

AESOP, AISOPOS: A writer of fables, perhaps legendary himself. He was reputed a native of Samos who flourished in the sixth century B.C.

AGAMEMNON: In mythology, commander-in-chief of the Greek forces at the siege of Troy.

AISCHINES: An indigent Athenian braggart, much given to boasting about his fabulous estates, as imaginary as Cloud-cuckooland.

AKESTOR: An Athenian tragic poet. See SAKAS.

ALKMENE: Wife of Amphitryon and mistress of Zeus by whom she became the mother of Herakles.

ALOPE: Mortal woman beloved by Poseidon.

AMMON: A celebrated shrine and oracle of Zeus in Libya.

AMPHION: Musician and husband of Niobe; at the touch of his lyre the stones rose from the ground and formed themselves together to make the ramparts of Thebes.

APHRODITE: Goddess of beauty and sexual love.

APOLLO: God of prophecy, music, healing, and light; his two chief shrines were at Delphoi (q.v.) and Delos (q.v.).

ARES: God of War.

ARISTOKRATES: Son of Skellias; a prominent Athenian politician of conservative persuasion. In 421 B.C. he was one of the signers of the Peace of Nikias between Athens and Sparta. In 411 he joined the moderate conservative Theramenes in setting up the government of the Four Hundred, but later withdrew.

ARTEMIS: Goddess of chastity, childbirth, and the hunt; sister of Apollo.

ATHENE, ATHENA: Patron goddess of Athens, commonly called "owl-eyed." Although a virgin goddess, she was also a goddess of war.

BABYLON: Ancient capital of Mesopotamia, situated on the Euphrates River. It was one of the largest cities of the ancient world, and among its wonders were its great brick walls, described by the historian Herodotos.

**BAKIS:**  A famous prophet of Boiotia, whose oracles were delivered in hexameter verse. In Aristophanes' comedies, the seers who cite Bakis are usually charlatans.

**BASILEIA:**  The personification of Empire and Sovereign Power; in the present version she appears as Miss Universe.

**CHAIREPHON:**  Friend and disciple of the philosopher Sokrates. His utter devotion to philosophy and the studious life and his striking pallor and emaciation made him a popular image of The Philosopher. Hence his nickname, The Bat or The Vampire.

**CHAOS:**  The nothingness or vacancy which existed before the creation of the world. In mythology Chaos was the mother of Erebos and Night.

**CHIANS:**  Inhabitants of the island of Chios, a state closely allied to Athens during the early Peloponnesian War and whose fidelity to the Athenian cause was rewarded by inclusion in the Athenian prayers for prosperity and success.

**DARIUS, DAREIOS:**  King of Persia (ruled 521-486 B.C.).

**DELOS:**  Small Aegean island sacred to Apollo.

**DELPHOI, DELPHI:**  A town in Phokis, celebrated for its great temple and oracle of Apollo.

**DEMETER:**  The Earth Mother; goddess of grain, agriculture, and the harvest, worshipped at her shrine at Eleusis in Attika.

**DIAGORAS:**  Poet and philosopher of Melos. Charged with atheism in Athens and condemned to death, he fled the city.

**DIEITREPHES:**  A notorious social climber. Of doubtful Athenian origin, he began his public career as a worker in wicker and a basketmaker, and gradually made his way upward in the military hierarchy. In 413 a detachment of Thracians under his command went amok and massacred a school full of children at Mykalessos.

**DODONA:**  An ancient oracle of Zeus in the mountains of Epiros.

**EPOPS:**  The Hoopoe, Tereus (q.v.).

**ETNA, AITNA:**  A city situated on a spur of the Sicilian mountain of the same name, founded by Hiero of Syracuse.

**EXEKESTIDES:**  Evidently a foreign slave of Karian extraction who succeeded in passing himself off as an Athenian citizen, i.e., the sort of man who would be at home anywhere.

GORGIAS: Of Leontini, a noted sophist and teacher of rhetoric.

HEBROS: A river of Thrace.

HERA: Consort of Zeus.

HERAKLES: Hero and demigod, son of Zeus and Alkmene, renowned for his great labors, prodigious strength, and equally prodigious appetite. Because Herakles is *par excellence* the monster-killer, it is particularly appropriate to swear by him when confronted by the monstrous, prodigious, freakish, or strange.

HERMES: The messenger god of Olympos; also god of thieves and the guide of the underworld.

HESTIA: Goddess of the hearth (and among Birds, goddess of the nest).

HIERO: Famous tyrant of Syracuse in Sicily, celebrated by the poet Pindar.

HIPPONIKOS: A common name in a wealthy and aristocratic Athenian family.

HOMER: The great epic poet of Greece, author of the *Iliad* and *Odyssey*.

HYMEN: God of marriage.

IKAROS: Son of the craftsman Daidalos, who escaped from Krete with his father by means of homemade wings of wax and feathers. But when Ikaros flew too high, the sun melted the wax, his wings dissolved, and he fell to his death in the sea.

IRIS: Messenger of the gods; in the earlier poets represented as a virgin.

ITYS: The son of Tereus and Prokne (q.v.), murdered by his mother in revenge for Tereus' rape and mutilation of Philomela. To the Greek ear, the name Itys seemed to form part of the refrain of the mourning nightingale.

KALLIAS: Common name in a wealthy and aristocratic Athenian family. The Kallias singled out here was a notorious profligate and spendthrift.

KINESIAS: A clubfooted dithyrambic poet of great pretensions but little ability.

KLEISTHENES: A notorious Athenian homosexual and one of Aristophanes' favorite butts.

KLEONYMOS: A corpulent glutton and part-time informer; he is Aristophanes' commonest representative of cowardice (i.e., throwing one's shield away).

KOLONOS: Small town on a hill near Athens; here the astronomer Meton (q.v.) had evidently constructed a complicated piece of engineering or clockwork.

KORINTH:   Greek city allied to Sparta during the Peloponnesian War; situated on the strategic Isthmus of Korinth.

KORKYRA:   Modern Corfu, a large island off the western coast of Greece. "Korkyrean wings" means "whip."

KRONOS:   Father of Zeus.

KYBELE:   A Phrygian Mother Goddess, worshipped as The Great Mother, "mother of gods and men."

LAURIUM, LAUREION:   In southeastern Attika, famous for its silver mines. Athenian silver coins, stamped with the owl of Athena, were commonly called "owls of Laureion."

LEOTROPHIDES:   An extremely fragile, delicate, and unsubstantial poet.

LEPREUS, LEPREUM:   A town in Elis; it recovered its independence from Elis during the Peloponnesian War.

LETO:   Mother of Artemis and Apollo.

LYDIA:   A region in Western Asia Minor which provided Athens with a large number of slaves.

LYKOURGOS:   An Athenian of sufficient distinction and/or oddity of appearance to have won the nickname of The Ibis. In this translation, however, he appears as The Lame Duck.

MANES:   A lazy slave.

MANODOROS:   A slave.

MARATHON:   A plain in the eastern part of Attika; site of the famous battle (490 B.C.) in which the Athenian forces under Miltiades crushingly defeated the first Persian invasion of Hellas.

MEIDIAS:   A venal and corrupt Athenian informer, evidently also a quail-breeder in his own right, whence his nickname, The Quail. For Aristophanes the propriety of the name is confirmed by Meidias' habitually dazed expression, like that of a freshly stunned quail.

MELANTHIOS:   Son of Philokles and, like his father, an atrocious tragedian. Afflicted with leprosy, he seems to have been also a noted glutton (cf. *Peace*, 804).

MENELAOS:   Mythological king of Sparta and brother of Agamemnon.

MENIPPOS:   An Athenian horse-raiser, nicknamed The Swallow (from a pun on the word *chelidon* which means both "swallow" and the tender "hollow" in a horse's hoof).

METON:   An Athenian astronomer, geometrician, and city-planner of considerable notoriety (see KOLONOS). According to Plutarch, Meton objected to the Sicilian expedition and pretended madness in order to keep his son at home.

NIKIAS: Prominent Athenian general during the Peloponnesian War. Enormously respected at Athens during his lifetime, Nikias' caution, slowness to move, stiffness, and superstitious piety were among the chief causes for the defeat of the Sicilian expedition. But as a cautious strategist and tactician, he had no equal among the Athenian generals.

ODYSSEUS: Hero of the *Odyssey* of Homer.

OLOPHYXIANS: Inhabitants of Olophyxos, a small town on the peninsula of Akte in Thrace.

OLYMPOS: A mountain in Thessaly, covered at the peak with perpetual snow and regarded by the Greeks as the abode of the gods.

OPOUNTIOS: A notorious one-eyed sycophant nicknamed The Crow.

OPOUS: A town in Lokris, whose inhabitants were called the Opuntian Lokrians.

ORESTES: A notorious burglar and highwayman; not to be confused with the heroic son of Agamemnon.

PAIAN: Manifestation of Apollo as god of healing.

PAN: Rural Arcadian god of the flocks and the woodlands.

PANDORA: Mother Earth, the giver of all gifts (*pan*, all; *dora*, gifts); not to be confused with the mythological mischief-maker and her box of human troubles.

PARIS: Prince of Troy; in the famous judgment of Paris, he was offered the most beautiful woman in the world by Aphrodite in return for awarding her the prize for beauty.

PEGASOS: The famous winged horse of mythology.

PEISANDROS: A notorious Athenian coward.

PEISIAS: Otherwise unknown, but evidently a noted traitor in his day.

PHILOKLES: Athenian tragic poet and nephew of Aischylos; among his lost plays was one which treated the story of Tereus and was evidently plagiarized from Sophokles' play of the same name. His nickname was The Lark because, according to the Scholiast, his head tapered like the pointed crest of that bird.

PHILOKRATES: An Athenian bird-seller.

PHLEGRA: A plain in Thrace said to have been the site of the great battle between the Gods and the Giants.

PHOIBOS:  Apollo.

PHRYGIA:  A country in central Asia Minor.

PINDAR:  Great lyric poet of Thebes (518-438 B.C.).

PORPHYRION:  Name of one of the Titans who fought against Zeus in the Battle of the Gods and the Giants; it is also the name of a bird, the Purple Waterhen.

POSEIDON:  Brother of Zeus and god of the sea. As sea-god, he girdles the earth and has it in his power as Poseidon Earth-Shaker to cause earthquakes. In still another manifestation he is Poseidon Hippios, patron god of horses and horsemen.

PRIAM:  King of Troy.

PRODIKOS:  Of Keos, a famous sophist.

PROKNE:  The nightingale, wife of Tereus (q.v.).

PROMETHEUS:  The great Titan who championed the cause of mankind against Zeus. Because he stole fire from heaven and gave it to men, he was regarded by the gods as a traitor to Olympos. His name means Foresight and his cleverness and philanthropy were both proverbial.

PROXENIDES:  An Athenian braggart and blowhard.

SAKAS:  The nickname of the Athenian tragic poet Akestor (q.v.). The word Sakas seems to be a pejorative for "Skyth" and presumably Akestor, like Exekestides, was a foreigner who had managed, or was reputed to have managed, to get his name entered on the citizenship rolls of Athens.

SEMELE:  Daughter of Kadmos of Thebes and mistress of Zeus, by whom she became the mother of Dionysos.

SIKYON:  Greek city situated on the northeast of the Peloponnesos, adjacent to Korinth.

SIMONIDES:  Of Keos, a lyric and elegiac poet (ca. 556-468 B.C.).

SKYTHS:  Savage nomadic inhabitants of Skythia, a region lying roughly between the Carpathians and the river Don.

SOKRATES:  The famous Athenian philosopher, ridiculed by Aristophanes for his long hair, bathlessness, and other philosophical traits.

SOLON:  Greatest of Athenian lawgivers (ca. 640-561 B.C.).

SOPHOKLES:  Athenian tragic poet (495-404 B.C.).

SYRAKOSIOS:  An extremely garrulous Athenian orator whose loquacity earned him the sobriquet of The Jaybird.

TARTAROS:  The great abyss which opened underneath Hades in the classical underworld.

TELEAS: Flighty and irresponsible Athenian bureaucrat; secretary to the Committee in charge of the Parthenon treasury.

TEREUS: In mythology, a son of Ares and king of the Daulians in Thrace. According to the legend, Pandion, king of Athens, had two daughters, Prokne and Philomela. Prokne was married to Tereus, by whom she became the mother of a son, Itys. Tereus, however, became infatuated with Prokne's sister Philomela, raped her, and cut out her tongue to keep her from informing Prokne. But Philomela managed to embroider her story in needlework and sent it to Prokne who, in retaliation against her husband, murdered her son Itys and served him up to Tereus for dinner. When he discovered the truth, Tereus pursued Prokne and Philomela but, before he could catch them, he was transformed into a Hoopoe, Prokne into a Nightingale, and Philomela into the Swallow. (In the better known but less appropriate Latin version of the myth, Philomela is the nightingale and Prokne the swallow).

   The story of Tereus was tragically treated by both Sophokles and Philokles.

THALES: Of Miletos, one of the Seven Sages of antiquity; renowned for his scientific genius and for having predicted an eclipse of the sun (ca. 636-546 B.C.).

THEBES: The principal city of Boiotia; during the Peloponnesian War an ally of Sparta.

THEOGENES: An Athenian braggart; probably took part with Kleon in the blockade of Sphakteria and was one of the signers of the Peace of Nikias in 421 B.C.

TIMON: The misanthrope *par excellence*.

TITANS: The race of pre-Olympian deities, born of Heaven and Earth. After the coming of the Olympians, the Titans rebelled against Zeus and were vanquished in the Battle of the Gods and the Giants at Phlegra.

TRIBALLOI: A savage people of Thrace. The name Triballos is merely an eponym of this people.

ZEUS: Chief god of the Olympian pantheon; son of Kronos, brother of Poseidon, and father of Athena. As the supreme ruler of the world, he is armed with thunder and lightning and creates storms and tempests.

## Other MENTOR Books of Interest

☐ **THE GREEK PHILOSOPHERS edited by Rex Warner.** Basic writings of philosophers from Thales to Plotinus.
(#MJ1716—$1.95)

☐ **THE ANCIENT MYTHS by Norma Lorre Goodrich.** A vivid retelling of the great myths of Greece, Egypt, India, Persia, Crete, Sumer, and Rome, capturing the beauty, vitality, and flavor of ancient cultures.
(#ME1714—$1.75)

☐ **GREAT DIALOGUES OF PLATO translated by W. H. D. Rouse.** A new translation into direct, forceful modern English of "The Republic" and other dialogues.
(#ME1803—$2.95)

☐ **THE ILIAD OF HOMER translated by W. H. D. Rouse.** Prose translation of Homer's great epic of the Trojan War, by a noted English scholar. (#MJ1923—$1.95)

☐ **THE ODYSSEY OF HOMER translated by W. H. D. Rouse.** A modern prose translation of the world's greatest adventure story, the travels of Ulysses.
(#MJ1943—$1.95)

☐ **THE OEDIPUS PLAYS OF SOPHOCLES translated by Paul Roche.** A dramatic new verse translation of "Oedipus the King," "Oedipus at Colonus," and "Antigone."
(#ME1964—$2.25)